©2023 Pokémon. ©1997–2019 Nintendo, Creatures, GAME FREAK, TV Tokyo, ShoPro, JR Kikaku. TM, ® Nintendo.

ISBN 978-1-338-87141-8

Originally published in Italian as *Ash e Pikachu Forever: Il Romanzo*
Translated by Emily Clement
Designed by Cheung Tai

10 9 8 7 6 5 4 3 2 1   23 24 25 26 27

Printed in the U.S.A.   40
First printing 2023

ASH AND PIKACHU'S ADVENTURES

Adapted by
Stefania Lepera

Scholastic Inc.

CONTENTS

ZOOM IN ON...

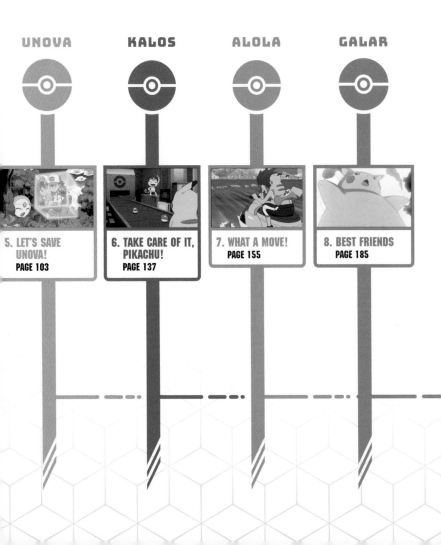

UNOVA

KALOS

ALOLA

GALAR

5. LET'S SAVE UNOVA!
PAGE 103

6. TAKE CARE OF IT, PIKACHU!
PAGE 137

7. WHAT A MOVE!
PAGE 155

8. BEST FRIENDS
PAGE 185

KANTO

1

I CHOOSE YOU!

CHAPTER 1
THE BEGINNING

It's not every day that you turn ten years old.

And if your dream is to become a Pokémon Trainer, then it's an especially important milestone. When you're ten, you can finally get your first Pokémon and set off on amazing adventures!

That's why Ash couldn't stand still that evening. He was pacing back and forth in his bedroom in anticipation.

He wanted to be sure that everything was ready for the next day: the beginning of a new stage of his life. He tried on the outfit he would wear, and as he placed his official Pokémon League Expo cap on his head, he felt invincible.

"I am Ash Ketchum from Pallet Town!" he declared, admiring himself in the mirror. "Now that I'm ten, I'll travel and learn all the secrets of Pokémon training."

Then he looked proudly at all his Pokémon—toy Pokémon, that is—and raised his voice to declare, "I will become the number one Trainer in the world. And one day I will be the greatest Pokémon Master of ALL TIME!"

"ASH, GO TO BED! NOW!"

Ash's mom, Delia, appeared at the door looking annoyed. Ash's confidence burst like a popped balloon.

"Do you know what time it is?" his mom asked. "Why are you still awake?"

"I can't sleep, Mom. Tomorrow is the big day!" Ash replied.

"I know, and that's exactly why you need to rest," his mom said. Then her eyes softened and she smiled. She knew just how her son was feeling, and she was just as excited as he was. "Watch Professor Oak's report, and then it's time for bed, okay?" his mom said, nodding to the TV showing the news.

"Okay," Ash agreed, then looked over at the screen with great interest.

The reporter had just turned it over to Professor Oak, a leading authority on Pokémon.

The Professor, a middle-aged man in a white coat, was standing in front of a picture of three Pokémon. "Good evening, everyone," he said. "Tomorrow, the new Pokémon students will have a big day. I have the pleasure of introducing you to Squirtle, Bulbasaur, and Charmander! All three are ready to work with their new Trainers. Which one of these magnificent Pokémon will each kid choose?"

"Which one will I choose?" Ash wondered, carefully studying the three Pokémon.

This question continued to buzz around in his head after he'd turned off the TV, while he put on his pajamas and got into bed. He didn't even stop thinking about it after he'd fallen asleep.

He dreamed that he was on a battlefield, and could see Bulbasaur, Charmander, and Squirtle in action. In his sleep, he reached out toward the Poké Ball–shaped alarm clock on his nightstand, grabbed it, and threw it, shouting, "Squirtle, I choose you!"

The alarm clock flew across the room and ended up crashing into the wall. Ash didn't notice a thing and continued the battle in his dream.

A few hours later, when Ash opened his eyes, he realized something wasn't right.

Light was coming in his window. Too much light!

He leaped out of bed with his heart in his throat and spotted the alarm clock in pieces on the floor. It took only a moment to put together what had happened during the night . . .

IT MUST BE SUPER LATE! he thought.

But there was no time to get upset. He needed to act quickly! He rushed to put on his shoes and then ran toward Professor Oak's laboratory.

"Squirtle, Charmander, Bulbasaur . . . any of them would work!" he said to himself as he ran, breathing heavily. "Just please save one for me! I'm comiiiiing!"

When he reached the lab, Professor Oak was waiting for him with a stern look. But his expression changed to confusion as he studied Ash from head to toe.

It was only then that Ash realized he was still in his pajamas!

Embarrassed, Ash chuckled. "There was just a little accident and . . . um . . . I'm a little late," he tried to explain. "But now I'm ready to get my Pokémon!"

"Your Pokémon?" the Professor said, raising an eyebrow.

That didn't sound very encouraging, but Ash didn't give up. "I thought about it all night long," he said, following the professor into the lab. "And in the end, I decided on Squirtle."

"I'm sorry, but Squirtle was already taken by a boy who was on time," the Professor replied.

"Oh . . . well, then . . . I'll take Bulbasaur!"

"That one was also taken by a boy who was on time."

"And Ch-Charmander?"

"The same."

"Then . . . all the Pokémon have already been taken?!" Ash was quickly losing all hope.

"Well, actually, there is one left," the Professor said, hesitating. "But . . ."

Ash didn't give him time to explain. "I want it!" he declared.

Meanwhile, they had reached the heart of the lab. The Professor took a Poké Ball and held it toward Ash.

Ash barely paid him any attention. This was a historic moment. He held his breath as he held out his hands to take the little ball. His first Poké Ball, his first Pokémon, his first step on a great journey! He should have given a speech in honor of the occasion, but there was no time.

As soon as Ash's hands closed around the Poké Ball, it opened, letting out a powerful burst of light that completely blinded him.

When the light dimmed, he saw a small yellow creature with lively black eyes and a tail shaped like a lightning bolt.

"*Pikachu!*" the Pokémon said in a sweet little voice.

It was Pikachu, the Mouse Pokémon, an Electric type. For Ash, it was love at first sight.

"It's so cute!" he said. "This is the best Pokémon of all! Oh, Pikachu!" he cried, picking it up and hugging it close.

Pikachu, however, did not seem to return Ash's affection, and did not appreciate the hug. Its cheeks began to sizzle—then Ash was struck by a powerful electric shock, like he'd stuck his finger in an outlet.

"Ow! Ow! Ow!" he shouted as electricity shot through his body.

Professor Oak was watching calmly. He explained, "This Pokémon is a bit shy, and has a rather *electrifying* personality."

"Message received," Ash said miserably when the shock finally ended.

The professor continued, "Now take these: your Pokédex and your Poké Balls—"

But as soon as Ash touched the professor's hand, a second electric shock even more powerful than the first burst from Pikachu's body, jolting both humans!

Singed and in pain, Ash and Professor Oak left the lab, followed by Pikachu.

Waiting for them outside were Delia and a group of friends who had come to send off Ash. Surprised, he went up to his mother.

"Ash, I am so proud of you!" she said with a smile. "Your dream has come true, and now you can begin training Pokémon. But I'll miss you so much, my little one!" Ash's mom let out a deep sigh, then handed Ash a backpack. She continued, "I packed your slippers, pants, sweaters, underwear, a wool hat for when it's cold, a pair of rubber gloves for washing dishes, thread for mending—"

Just then, she noticed Pikachu at her son's feet. "Oh, how cuuuute! Is this your Pokémon?"

"*Pi!*" said Pikachu, tilting its head to the side.

"Yes, that's it," Ash replied.

"I thought that Pokémon all stayed in their Poké Balls. Why is it outside?" asked his mom.

"Yeah, that's true," said Ash. "Pikachu, get in!" he commanded, tossing the Poké Ball toward it. Pikachu just batted the ball away with its tail.

Ash tried again and again, but with the same result: he threw the Poké Ball and Pikachu sent it right back to him.

"Oh, you're playing!" his mom said. "You're already becoming friends!"

"That's right," Ash said, giving up on the Poké Ball and picking up Pikachu. "We're best friends."

Watching them closely, his mom commented, "That's a strange Pokémon, though."

Pikachu squinted its eyes and lowered its ears. Evidently, it didn't like this observation.

Before Ash could do anything, his Pokémon exploded into a third electric shock that jolted everyone around him.

This isn't going to be easy, Ash thought. Every cell of his body sizzled like a french fry in hot oil!

CHAPTER 2

A STORMY START

Tied to a leash, Pikachu was forced to follow Ash. They were on a path in the countryside outside Pallet Town.

However much Pikachu dug in its little paws, though, it couldn't avoid being dragged ahead by its young Trainer. And Ash had to put in a lot of effort to pull his stubborn companion.

At one point, the boy stopped to catch his breath and kneeled down next to the Pokémon.

"You're doing this because you don't like me, huh?" he asked sadly.

"*Pika, pi,*" Pikachu replied, nodding.

"Okay." Ash sighed. He untied the rope around Pikachu's middle. "Maybe now you'll feel better."

Pikachu's body seemed to relax, but its expression remained stubborn and hostile.

Just then, a sound drew their attention. A Pidgey was pecking in the grass nearby. Ash immediately activated his Pokédex, which recited in a robotic voice: "Among all Flying-type Pokémon, Pidgey is the easiest to catch. Ideal for beginning Trainers."

"Perfect!" Ash cried. "This is our lucky day. Pikachu, go get it!"

Pikachu stayed exactly where it was and let out a "*Pi*" of disapproval.

"Have you decided not to listen to me?" Ash asked, discouraged. How would he ever catch new Pokémon if Pikachu refused to work with him?

To show just how little it was interested in battles, Pikachu ran over to a nearby tree, scrambled up onto a branch, made itself comfortable, and yawned.

"Do what you want. I don't need you," Ash said. "I can get that Pokémon on my own!"

Well aware that Pikachu was watching, Ash grabbed one of his empty Poké Balls and, as he'd seen his heroes on TV do a thousand times before, threw it in the direction of the Tiny Bird Pokémon.

"Poké Ball, go!"

The Pidgey couldn't avoid the Poké Ball, and disappeared inside with a flash of light.

"I did it!" cheered Ash, leaping with joy.

But he had claimed victory too soon.

The Poké Ball started to shake, then it burst open, letting the Pidgey escape into the grass.

"*Pi-hee-hee,*" Pikachu giggled, enjoying the scene from its branch.

"You could give me a hand instead of laughing!" Ash grumbled.

Angry but not discouraged, he rummaged through his backpack to find something useful for catching the Pokémon. He grabbed his pajamas and thought, *Here we go!*

Ash quietly began to search for the Pidgey. When he spotted it, he flung his pajamas onto it, covering it completely.

"You have to be my friend!" Ash shouted, grabbing the Pidgey. It struggled against him, but it could tell that Ash wasn't going to loosen his grip. So the Pokémon attacked: a Gust burst from its wings and pushed Ash over. Then, as the Pidgey took flight, its Sand Attack hit Ash right in the face.

"*Pi-hee-hee*," Pikachu giggled again.

Now Ash was truly furious. This was not how he'd imagined his first day as a Trainer!

To let out his anger, he grabbed a stone and threw it in the direction of another Pidgey he glimpsed in the grass. Only after he had thrown it did he realize that the color of the Pokémon's feathers was different from the first Pidgey. In fact, after getting a better look, he realized that this wasn't another Pidgey.

"What could it be?" Ash wondered.

His Pokédex responded.

"Spearow, the Tiny Bird Pokémon. Unlike Pidgey, it has a bad attitude. It is very wild and will sometimes attack other Pokémon—and humans!"

As if to confirm this description, the angry Spearow flew into the air, then dove back down in an attack. Ash was forced to throw himself on the ground to avoid the Spearow's sharp talons.

Then the Spearow saw Pikachu seated on the branch and flew over to attack it instead.

"Hey, leave it alone! It has nothing to do with this!" Ash shouted to the Spearow.

Luckily, Pikachu knew how to defend itself, and it struck the Spearow with one of its tremendous electric shocks.

The Spearow fell to the grass. Ash's reflexes weren't quick enough to throw a Poké Ball at it in time, and the

Pokémon let out a loud call. Quick as a flash, a whole flock of Spearow appeared out of a nearby tree.

"I think we'd better get out of here!" Ash said to Pikachu.

"*Pika pi*," it replied. For once, they were in agreement.

Unfortunately, it's not easy to escape an angry flock of flying Pokémon. No matter how quickly they ran, Ash and Pikachu weren't able to lose the Spearow.

Some of them soon caught up to Pikachu and started pecking and poking it mercilessly.

"No, Pikachu!" Ash shouted, seeing his companion in trouble. Without thinking twice, he threw himself at the Mouse Pokémon to protect it with his own body, and managed to keep it away from the ferocious beaks of the Spearow.

By that point, however, Pikachu had fainted. Ash took it in his arms and started running again, with the Spearow flock still close behind.

His escape was suddenly interrupted when he reached the edge of a cliff. Far below him, a river churned. Above him, the Spearow prepared for a new attack.

"I have no other choice," Ash said hopelessly. "I have to jump!"

With Pikachu held tightly in his arms, the boy let out a yell and leaped into the river.

The foaming water swallowed him up, and the strong current carried him away.

Up ahead, the riverbed widened and the flow of water was slower and calmer. A girl was sitting on the riverbank fishing, hoping to catch a Magikarp. Suddenly, her fishing line jerked. Something was hooked!

The girl jumped to her feet and pulled as hard as she

could. "It must be huge!" she shouted, grinding her teeth with the effort. Giving it her all, she managed to drag her catch to the shore . . . but instead of a Magikarp or a Gyarados, she found a boy clutching a yellow Pokémon.

After she recovered from her surprise, the girl asked gently, "Are you okay?"

"Y-yes, thanks," Ash replied, coughing.

"Not you!" the girl responded. "I was talking to your Pokémon. Just look at it! Is it still breathing?"

"I think so." Ash looked over at Pikachu. His companion was still passed out, and looked pained.

"Don't just sit there!" the girl shouted. "This Pokémon

needs medical attention. There's a Pokémon Center near here. You have to go there right away!"

"Could you show me the way?" Ash asked.

She pointed toward it.

Ash was just about to start running again when he saw the flock of Spearow appear on the horizon. Those creatures didn't give up! Without thinking twice, Ash jumped onto a bicycle parked nearby and put Pikachu in the basket.

"Hey!" shouted the girl. "What are you doing? That's my bike!"

"Sorry, but it's an emergency," said Ash. "I'll bring it back to you!"

All the girl could do was watch him go, disappearing among the trees in the distance.

Ash pedaled as fast as he could, both to get away from the Spearow and to get to the Pokémon Center as quickly as possible. In the basket, Pikachu's eyes were half-closed and it was having difficulty breathing. Clearly it wasn't doing very well.

Meanwhile, the sky had filled with heavy gray clouds.

Rain soon started to fall, complete with thunder and flashes of lightning.

But this still didn't discourage the Spearow, who were closer to Ash than ever!

His eyes blurred with rain, Ash didn't notice a big rock in the middle of the road, and ran the bike right into it. He took a terrible fall off the bike, and Pikachu was tossed out of the basket and into the mud.

After struggling to get up, Ash rushed over to his Pokémon. He saw that its eyes were still half open, but it couldn't move.

"Pikachu, please, get into your Poké Ball," the boy begged, taking out the ball.

Now Ash's eyes were blurred with tears instead of rain. "I know that you don't like staying inside it, but if you go in, I'll be able to save you. Please, you have to trust me!"

"*Pika* . . ." Pikachu murmured weakly.

A flutter of wings made Ash turn. The Spearow were there, ready to strike!

"Hey, Spearow, maybe you don't know who's in front of you," Ash shouted. "I am destined to become the greatest Pokémon Master in the world, and I will defeat you all!"

Pikachu gently lifted its head, struck by Ash's tone. There was determination and courage in his voice. But above all, the young Trainer had also shown affection and loyalty, even though Pikachu had been so grumpy with him.

And now he was facing down those Spearow to protect Pikachu, when he could easily have found shelter under the trees by himself instead.

"Come on, I'm ready!" Ash shouted.

The flock zoomed toward the boy. Suddenly, Pikachu took action. Calling on all its energy, the little Pokémon

got up, ran to Ash, and scrambled onto his shoulder. From there, it leaped forward just as a bolt of lightning flashed in the sky.

The Electric-type Pokémon's body attracted the lightning and multiplied its power. Pikachu let loose a mighty Thunder Shock that sent the Spearow flock away for good.

The shockwave was so strong that both Ash and Pikachu crumpled to the ground, stunned.

About a half hour later, when Ash came to, the sun was shining once again. The bicycle, now totally charred, lay a few steps away. Pikachu was right by his side.

The Pokémon also opened its eyes. Looking at Ash, it let out a feeble "*Pikachu.*" There was something different in its expression now. Instead of looking cold and hostile, it held the promise of being a good partner and friend.

Ash saw the change, and it warmed his heart.

But right now, the most important thing was to get to the Pokémon Center. Pikachu needed medical care as soon as possible!

CHAPTER 3

EMERGENCY!

With Pikachu in his arms, Ash finally reached Viridian City. He was exhausted from the long journey, but all he could think about was saving his friend.

Ash was so focused on his goal that he didn't hear the announcement over the city's loudspeakers. However, he should have listened carefully, because it was very worrying news.

"Attention!" a woman's voice said. "Attention! Pokémon thieves have been detected in the city. Secure your Pokémon and report anyone suspicious to the authorities!"

Officer Jenny had just pushed away the microphone after making the announcement when she saw a boy rush by with a Pokémon in his arms. His disheveled appearance seemed suspicious, so she ordered him to halt.

"Where do you think you're going?" Officer Jenny said. "Show me your papers."

"Huh? What?" Ash didn't understand. "What papers? I . . . I have to take my Pokémon to the hospital!" he spluttered.

He was so confused and desperate-looking, Officer Jenny realized he was telling the truth.

"I see," she said. "Come on, I'll take you there."

She jumped onto her motorcycle and motioned for Ash to get into the sidecar, then hit the gas and took off. A few minutes later, the motorcycle drove right into the lobby of the Pokémon Center.

The nurse was astonished. "Hey!" she protested. "What kind of manners are these?"

"It's an emergency, Nurse Joy!" Officer Jenny explained. "This Pokémon is badly hurt!"

Ash's legs shook as he got out of the sidecar, after Officer Jenny's wild driving. Pikachu moaned weakly in his arms.

Nurse Joy didn't waste a moment and put through emergency orders. Right away, two Chansey appeared, pushing a stretcher. Ash gently lay Pikachu down.

"It'll be in good shape soon," Nurse Joy reassured him.

Then, Nurse Joy turned to the Chansey. "Take this Pikachu to intensive care."

"If I can help in any way . . ." Ash said with a lump in his throat.

"It's our responsibility now. You stay here," the nurse replied, rushing after the stretcher.

The door closed behind her and a red light on the wall turned on.

When Officer Jenny

had left, too, Ash found himself all alone in the Pokémon Center's lobby. Sitting in a corner with his head down, there was nothing he could do but wait—and the wait seemed endless. Minutes became hours, but the red light remained on. Ash tried to overcome his anxiety, but he felt tremendous guilt. If only he had been more careful! He should never have reacted so angrily toward that Spearow.

"The job of a Trainer is to take care of their Pokémon, not expose them to needless danger," he told himself.

His journey had just begun, and he had already landed in a sea of trouble!

Ash remembered how the girl by the river had looked at him as she fished him out of the water. Her expression had said, "It's all your fault! Look how you've ended up!"

Strangely, Ash felt as though he was actually hearing the girl's voice saying that.

"Hey, I'm talking to you!"

That voice wasn't just in his head. It was real!

Ash looked up and was shocked to see the girl from the river right in front of him, looking furious. The wrecked bicycle was hoisted onto her shoulders.

"I knew I'd find you here," she said. "Now you owe me for the bike!"

"I'm so sorry," said Ash solemnly. "I'll fix it, I promise. But I *had* to save Pikachu, remember?" Then, looking for the thousandth time at the red light on the wall, he added sadly, "It's badly hurt!"

The girl could see that Ash was miserable, and her anger evaporated. She was just thinking of something comforting to say when the red light for intensive care was turned off.

The waiting room door opened, and Nurse Joy reappeared with the stretcher. On it was Pikachu: its eyes were closed but it was breathing steadily.

"Pikachu!" shouted Ash, running over.

"It's resting now," the nurse informed him. "The treatment is working and it will recover soon."

"Thank you!" cried Ash, almost in tears with relief. "Thank you, thank you, thank you!"

"It's no trouble," Nurse Joy said. Then, noticing the girl with the charred bicycle on her shoulders, she asked, "And who are you?"

"My name is Misty. And I'm here because *he* destroyed my bike!"

"Again, I'm sorry!" Ash said once more. "At least Pikachu will recover—"

But he was interrupted by the sound of breaking glass. Two Poké Balls crashed through the window and landed on the floor of the Pokémon Center!

The balls opened with a flash of light, revealing an Ekans and a Koffing. The Koffing released a thick, black cloud of smoke that filled the room and made everyone cough.

It all happened so quickly that no one had time to react.

"What's going on?" asked Ash, pinching his nose.

"Don't be afraid, little boy," an unpleasant voice said, and the outlines of a teenage boy and girl emerged from behind the curtain of smoke.

"Allow us to introduce ourselves," the boy said. "I am James."

"And I am Jessie," added the girl. "We are Team Rocket! And you have no way out."

"Surrender!" added a Pokémon that appeared between them. A talking Pokémon! It was a Meowth, and he looked just as evil as his human companions.

Nurse Joy knew that these had to be the Pokémon thieves from Officer Jenny's announcement earlier.

"You're wasting your time," she said. "You'll only find sick and injured Pokémon here."

"That may be," Jessie replied acidly, "But I wouldn't be surprised to find some rare and precious Pokémon among these useless wrecks."

Ash didn't like this Team Rocket one bit. "You're starting to annoy me!" he cried, feeling ready to fight them with his bare hands. But as much as he wanted to, what could one boy do against a group of dangerous criminals?

Nothing, unfortunately. The best idea was to find shelter before Ekans and Koffing could attack again!

Nurse Joy, Ash, and Misty took Pikachu and shut themselves into a large room. It was almost like a library, but the shelves were filled with Poké Balls rather than books.

Ash barely had a chance to look around before everything turned dark.

"They shut off the power!" cried Misty.

"Never fear," said Nurse Joy. "We have emergency 'Pika Power'!"

The lights turned back on a moment later, thanks to a dozen Pikachu nearby! They were running in circles on a disc connected to a generator, creating energy.

Ash and Misty saw the Electric-type Pikachu in action and wanted to know more about them, but Nurse

Joy had rushed to the control panel of a big machine. "We must save the Pokémon!" she shouted.

A long mechanical arm with a claw on the end began to grab Poké Balls from the shelves and drop them into an enormous metal funnel. From there, the machine transported the balls to the Pokémon Center in Pewter City. But there were too many Poké Balls, and Nurse Joy hadn't managed to send off even half of them when the door to the room crashed open.

It was Team Rocket!

Misty acted right away. "Save Pikachu," she commanded Ash. "I'll take care of those three scoundrels."

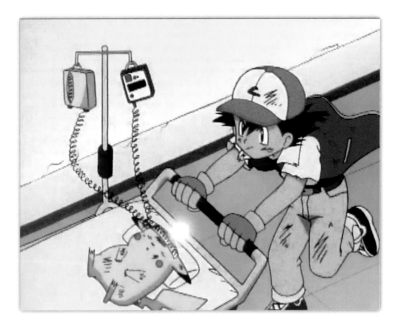

Stepping forward bravely, she took out her Poké Ball and threw it toward Team Rocket.

When the ball opened, however, a Goldeen emerged—a Water-type Pokémon that couldn't battle out of the water! Misty tried to call it back into its Poké Ball before Koffing and Ekans could attack, while Jessie and James burst out laughing.

Okay, maybe Misty's move didn't work, but at least it had given Ash time to escape!

Pushing Pikachu's stretcher, Ash ran toward the Pokémon Center's exit. A part of him wanted to stay

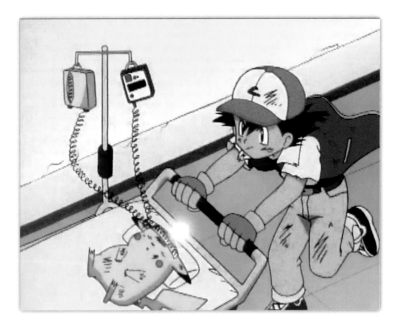

and fight, but he knew that his primary responsibility was to protect his Pokémon.

However, his escape was interrupted when the stretcher crashed right into Misty's bike, which had been abandoned on the floor. The bump woke up Pikachu, which opened its eyes in time to see Team Rocket running in their direction.

Pikachu knew that it had to do something, but it was still too weak.

"Pika, pika!" it murmured in a daze, looking up at Ash.

A moment later, as if called by its cry, all the Pikachu of the Pika Power machine rushed over and jumped onto the stretcher! Powerful, dazzling bolts of electricity coursed out of their bodies and hit Team Rocket.

What a shock! Jessie and James were fried, and Koffing and Ekans were totally knocked out.

As soon as the shocks had stopped, Ash's Pikachu emerged from the little group of Mouse Pokémon, perfectly healed. The current generated by the others had restored its energy!

"Pikachu!" shouted Ash, surprised and happy to see his friend recovered.

"*Pika, pika!*" it responded enthusiastically.

But the battle wasn't over yet. Meowth had stayed apart from the rest of Team Rocket and hadn't been struck by the electricity. Now the Scratch Cat Pokémon was advancing threateningly toward them.

"I'll take care of this!" Meowth cried. "Come here, little mice."

"*Pika pika, pika pika,*" said Pikachu, turning to Ash.

"What?" Ash asked. He didn't understand Pokémon language, but he knew Pikachu was trying to tell

him something. He and Pikachu tried to communicate without words.

"Of course—you need more energy!" Ash finally understood. Right away, he had an idea for how to help.

Ash jumped onto the seat of Misty's bike and began to pedal with all his might. The bike was wrecked and couldn't move, but the energy from the pedaling still lit up the light on the handlebars. Pikachu jumped on, and its body filled with the electric current. Soon it had taken in enough electricity to attack. It launched a huge Thunder Shock at Team Rocket.

This time, no one could hide, not even the crafty Meowth. The shock was so powerful that when the electricity subsided, the three criminals barely had the strength to escape.

"We were beaten by a mouse!" cried Jessie, as they limped away.

Meowth observed, "That Pikachu isn't like the others!"

"Yeah, it's a unique Pokémon. The perfect target!" said James.

"One day we'll catch it!" Jessie declared.

Now that they had their sights set on Pikachu, there was no telling what those three would do in the future.

For the moment, though, the danger was over. Ash and Pikachu had won their first battle together! And they had done it because they trusted each other as partners, just as a Trainer and their Pokémon always should.

ZOOM IN ON . . .

There are lots of villains who Ash and Pikachu face together in their adventures. Often, these characters belong to criminal gangs. Here are some of the evil groups they've encountered!

TEAM AQUA

In the Hoenn region, Team Aqua tries to take control of the Legendary Pokémon Kyogre and dominate the seas with it. In their attempts to put their evil plan into action, they battle with Team Magma.

TEAM MAGMA

Rivals of Team Aqua, Team Magma wants to catch the Legendary Pokémon Groudon to take advantage of its power over dry land. But neither of the two criminal groups know what's coming when they deal with Ash and Pikachu!

TEAM GALACTIC

Team Galactic thinks big and thinks bad! Their absurd goal is to transform the entire universe by forcing the Legendary Pokémon Dialga and Palkia to work for them! What could be worse than that?

MORE THAN TEAM ROCKET!

TEAM PLASMA

The goal of Team Plasma is simple: take control of all Pokémon in the Unova region, and certainly not for good reasons! The evil scientist Colress developed a machine that allows him to control the minds of Pokémon and make them very violent. It's extremely dangerous!

TEAM FLARE

How do you eliminate all the evils of humanity? According to Team Flare, the solution is simple: eliminate humanity entirely! The only people allowed to survive will be those who join their team. Will these villains manage to capture Zygarde to use the energy from its Mega Evolution?

TEAM SKULL

A paradise like Alola doesn't deserve a band of troublemakers like Team Skull. These hooligans don't have any kind of real plan in mind: they just want to create chaos and steal Pokémon.

JOHTO

2

ALL FOR ONE, ONE FOR ALL

The sun was shining. It was a beautiful day in the Johto region, and Ash was walking along a path in the countryside with Misty and Brock.

They all began to smell something delightful. It was ripe apples! There was an orchard just over a small hill, and the inviting scent was wafting over.

Curious, Pikachu jumped down from Ash's shoulder and scurried to the orchard. It soon disappeared from sight.

A minute later, when the friends reached the trees, they found Pikachu surrounded by apple cores. It looked like it had enjoyed quite a feast!

"I'm surprised at you, Pikachu," Brock scolded it. "You shouldn't have eaten those apples without permission. Clearly this orchard belongs to someone."

"Pika! Pika! Pika!" cried Pikachu, annoyed at the accusation.

"I doubt that Pikachu would have done such a thing," said Ash. "It would never steal anything from anyone!"

The little Pokémon nodded and started gesticulating wildly to try to make them understand ... but suddenly a net fell on it, trapping it! A moment later, a young woman ran up to Pikachu and glared at it.

"Excellent! I've got you at last!" she said. "So you're the little thief who's been eating my apples, huh? It's time to stop!"

Brock, who never missed an opportunity to talk to a charming girl, stepped up to say sorry ... and to flirt.

"I want to apologize on behalf of Pikachu," he said, giving her a gentlemanly bow. "I don't know what got into it. Usually—"

"Hey, wait a minute!" Ash interrupted. "Pikachu isn't a thief. I can prove it, too!"

He grabbed a gnawed apple core from the ground and asked Pikachu to open its mouth.

"Look at the size of these bites," Ash said. He motioned for the others to come closer. "Pikachu's teeth would leave much bigger marks."

"That's true," the young woman admitted. "It couldn't be this Pokémon." She rushed to free it from the net. "I'm sorry I accused you, Pikachu. The fact is, I'm desperate, because something has been eating my apples for a while now. But I'm pleased to meet you! My name is Charmaine. Please, let me make it up to you by inviting you to lunch."

Ash and his friends accepted right away. Being around the apples had already made them hungry!

Charmaine led them through the large orchard to a beautiful farmhouse. She told them to make themselves comfortable while she prepared lunch.

Soon, while they ate, Charmaine went into more detail about her problem. "Normally the main threats to my harvest are Pidgey, and I try to keep them at bay with sound deterrents, such as wooden boards that move in the wind and make noise. Over the last few days, though, there's something that hasn't been scared away by the sound, and it's been stealing my apples. I work very hard, so it's disappointing to see something taking my harvest."

"I imagine that an orchard of this size would be a lot of work," Ash observed. "Do you take care of it all by yourself?"

Charmaine nodded. "Yes. I haven't found anyone who wants to work with me."

Ash exchanged a look with his friends, then continued, "Let us help you. We can give you a hand with harvesting apples. The more, the merrier!"

Charmaine didn't want to take advantage of her guests' kindness, but they insisted—especially Brock—and at last she agreed.

So, that very afternoon, the young woman handed out large baskets to Ash, Misty, and Brock, and they all went to the apple orchard.

They had barely begun to work when they heard a strange sound, as if wooden sticks were smacking into one another.

"My sound deterrents!" cried Charmaine. "There's something moving in the branches and setting them off!"

Pikachu's sensitive ears twitched, trying to locate the source of the noise. It ran to chase after the thief—or, rather, the thieves!

As Pikachu quickly discovered, it was three Pokémon very similar to Pikachu but smaller, leaping from branch to branch and snatching every apple they could.

Pikachu waited for them to reach the ground and then positioned itself right in front of them with its paws on its hips.

"*Pika, pika!*" it shouted. "*Pika. Pika. Pika!*"

"*Pichu,*" they sighed. They seemed to be embarrassed.

They murmured, "*Pichu, pichu,*" again as if to apologize, and led Pikachu toward their hiding place nearby. There, several even smaller Pokémon were huddled, trembling timidly. Pikachu realized that the apples were being taken for them.

Ash and the others arrived a few

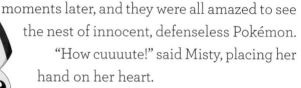

moments later, and they were all amazed to see the nest of innocent, defenseless Pokémon.

"How cuuuute!" said Misty, placing her hand on her heart.

Ash opened his Pokédex to learn about the Pokémon. "Pichu, the Tiny Mouse Pokémon," it said. "The pre-evolved form of Pikachu. In spite of its smaller size, it emits electric shocks that can harm human beings. It isn't able to control its own electrical power. If it's surprised or if it bursts out laughing, it can let out a shock by mistake and harm itself."

"How cuuuute!" Misty squealed again.

"So these are the apple thieves," Charmaine said, still surprised. "I thought it would be hooligans, and instead it's a family of sweet little creatures!"

The three largest Pichu walked up to her and placed the stolen apples at her feet.

"*Pichu pi-pi. Chuuuu,*" explained one of them. It seemed very sorry, and it was clear that it didn't like the idea of stealing.

Meanwhile, the other Pichu kept trembling and clinging to one another.

"They seem very hungry," Ash said.

"Maybe the fruits and berries that they usually eat in the forest are scarce, and that's why they came here," Charmaine suggested. "Their instincts guided them to a place full of food."

The little Pokémon were so gentle and cute that the orchard owner quickly came to a decision. "Go ahead, eat these apples. They're all for you!" she said.

Surprised and happy, the Pichu started devouring the apples, taking big bites. For such small creatures, they sure had big appetites!

The Pokémon had just finished their excellent meal when they all heard a loud noise from above. It was a flock of Pidgey pecking at the apples!

"Oh no!" cried Charmaine. "It's never-ending!"

"Pikachu, take care of it!" shouted Ash. He couldn't leave a friend in the lurch.

The Pidgey were very hungry and seemed determined

to chomp as many apples as possible. So Pikachu sprang into action and called on the Pichu for help.

"*Pika, pika, pika,*" it explained, and they immediately understood what to do.

With a few leaps, the Pichu were up in the trees. They gnashed their teeth and sent electric shocks toward the

Pidgey, which weakened them. Then the Pichu jumped on the Pidgey's backs and shocked them again.

The Tiny Bird Pokémon were overpowered. Even though they were hungry, they flew away.

"It worked!" Ash cried, clapping his hands.

Once the Pichu were back on the ground, they were showered with cheers and praise. Charmaine was particularly delighted. "Thank you! Thank you so much! You don't know how much work it is to keep away those creatures!"

Ash looked thoughtful. "I have an idea, Charmaine," he said. "The Pichu could stay with you and help you. Not just to keep away the Pidgey, but also because they're so good at gathering apples!"

"That's true! That's a great suggestion, Ash," Charmaine replied, laughing. Then she looked down at the little Pokémon and added, "I thought I was going to catch thieves, but instead I found helpers!"

"Yeah!" said Ash. "And I'm sure that you'll soon be good friends, just like Pikachu and me!"

Though Charmaine didn't know it yet, a much greater threat was coming to her orchard: Team Rocket had their eye on her apples!

Jessie, James, and Meowth were a troublemaking trio. But for all the wicked plans they put in motion, very few went perfectly—so they always needed more money. They decided that stealing Charmaine's apples and then selling them could be a big business for them!

While Ash and his friends were helping Charmaine,

the orchard was suddenly covered in a dark shadow. The friends looked up and saw a hot-air balloon that looked like Meowth floating above the trees.

Ash recognized Team Rocket right away. After their first encounter in Viridian City, he had run into them many times.

"You again? You're wasting your time!" he shouted. "You'll never manage to steal anything because we'll stop you!"

"I don't think so!" Jessie scoffed. "We have a super sucker!"

A trapdoor in the bottom of the balloon's basket opened and a long, flexible tube that looked like a giant vacuum was lowered over the trees, ready to suck up all the fruit.

But Ash wasn't scared. Just the fact that these three fools thought they could put their plan into action right in front of his eyes made him furious.

Pikachu had the same reaction, and the partners shared a look to communicate what they should do next. "Go!" said Ash.

Pikachu nodded, then ran up a tree and leaped toward their enemy, ready to strike. But it hadn't considered the power of the vacuum, which sucked the Pokémon up toward it. A moment later, Pikachu was stuck in the mouth of the vacuum tube!

Pikachu tried using its electricity to free itself, but each shock was absorbed by the metal tube and traveled up to charge the balloon's battery!

"Ha ha ha!" laughed Meowth. "Now we're at full power. Soon we'll take all the apples, and then we'll also take Pikachu!"

Pikachu had no intention of giving up so easily. It sent out shocks again and again, but soon, it was out of energy. After one last shock, it closed its eyes and fainted.

Ash was stuck on the ground, powerless. What could he do to save his friend, who was stuck so high in the air? He didn't have any Pokémon with him who could help!

Then even more vacuum tubes were lowered from the basket and started sucking up apples. Soon the trees would be empty.

But Team Rocket hadn't counted on the Pichu!

Seeing the orchard under such a great threat, the Tiny Mouse Pokémon decided to take action.

Brock was the first to notice them making their way up the tree trunks.

"The Pichu are planning to fight!" he shouted. "Look over there!"

The Pokémon had assembled at the top of one of the trees. Then they united their powers to let loose a huge Thunder Shock against the hot-air balloon. It gave Jessie, James, and Meowth a tremendous jolt!

However, the little Pokémon weren't able to keep up such a big fight for long, and soon their energy was exhausted.

Meowth immediately reversed the air on one of the vacuum tubes and blew the Pichu back down to the ground.

All hope now seemed to be lost for Charmaine:

Pikachu was still out of it, and the Pichu seemed too weak to fight.

But never underestimate a Pokémon, especially when they're trying to repay a human's generosity.

As soon as they had recovered, the Pichu went straight back up the trees, showing their determination. Then they climbed one on top of another to form a chain all the way up to Pikachu.

"They're creating an electric battery!" said Brock. "That way they can give Pikachu energy!"

Brock was right. When the last Pichu touched Pikachu's foot, the electricity flowed through their bodies and passed into the Mouse Pokémon, who immediately woke up.

"Pikachu!" shouted Ash. "Use Thunderbolt!"

The energy from the Thunderbolt and the Pichu combined and quickly passed up through the vacuum tube.

At first, Team Rocket cheered.

"Ha ha ha!" laughed Meowth. "Thank you, Pikachu. The more you attack us, the more supercharged our battery gets."

All the instruments on board the hot-air balloon were fully charged and running at full capacity.

But a moment later, the three troublemakers realized that their battery wasn't just charged, it was OVERCHARGED!

And then . . . *BOOOOM!*

The hot-air balloon lit up like a star, then exploded like a volcano. Team Rocket was blasted into the sky.

Another one of their evil plans had failed miserably!

"Nooooo! We're blasting off again!" the trio shouted, and disappeared over the horizon.

There was no question: when Team Rocket battled Ash and Pikachu, they were sure to lose.

Now Pikachu was finally free. It climbed down from the tree with the Pichu and rejoined Ash and the others.

"You were all wonderful!" cried Misty, clapping her hands.

"Good job! You're so small yet so brave!" Brock cheered.

"Ash, you were right," Charmaine added as she gave the Pichu a group hug. "I've found some wonderful friends!"

Ash and Pikachu shared a smile, happy with the way the day had ended. They knew how important it was to be able to count on your friends when facing any obstacle.

HOENN

3

A PERFECT PAIR

Ash and Pikachu had already lived through a sea of adventures together when they arrived in Rustboro City in the Hoenn region. They were there to face down Roxanne, the city's Gym Leader.

To prepare for the battle, Ash and Pikachu spent the morning practicing Iron Tail, a move that the Mouse Pokémon hadn't yet perfected.

After all their time together, Ash had learned one very important thing: For a Pokémon to do its best, it needed to have a strong bond with its Trainer. And there was more than just a strong bond between Pikachu and Ash—by now they couldn't live without each other!

Pikachu loved battling, and just like Ash, it never wanted to give up. Sometimes they won their battles, and sometimes they lost, but they always learned something new. The bond between the partners became deeper every day.

In Rustboro City, Ash was determined to earn the Stone Badge. It wouldn't be easy—the Gym Leader was a formidable Trainer with a lot of experience. Plus, she specialized in Rock-type Pokémon, which had an advantage over Electric-type Pokémon like Pikachu. Even so, Ash had a glint of fiery confidence in his eyes.

His friends Brock, Vera, and Max, who had accompanied him on his journey through the Hoenn region, recognized that spark—and also knew that Ash could end up burned by it.

Sometimes, his overconfidence could lead to bad choices. Would that happen again this time? The three friends looked forward to finding out as they took their places in the Gym's arena.

Roxanne met Ash on the battlefield, which was huge and scattered with boulders.

"Welcome, Ash!" she said. "Are you ready to begin?"

"Yes! I can't wait!"

"You seem awfully confident," Roxanne replied. "Good—this should be fun!"

The Gym's referee explained the rules. "This is an elimination battle. Each Trainer can use two Pokémon."

When he gave the signal, Roxanne called out Geodude, while Ash chose Treecko.

"Excellent choice on Ash's part," Max commented from the stands. "A Grass-type has an advantage over a Rock-type like Geodude."

"Yes, but there's one problem," Brock replied. "This Treecko doesn't know any Grass-type moves!"

Brock was right. Ash had met Treecko only a short time ago. The pair had quickly become friends, but they hadn't trained very much together, so the Wood Gecko Pokémon wasn't an expert at battle by any means.

"Oh no!" said Vera. "What's Ash's strategy, then?"

As if in response, Ash told Treecko to begin

a Quick Attack. The Pokémon launched itself toward its opponent, but Geodude had no problem stopping the attack. It was too strong to be beaten in a hand-to-hand fight.

At Roxanne's signal, Geodude fired off a Mega Punch that sent Treecko high into the air. Ash seemed to have been waiting for that very moment, and yelled, "Perfect! Now use Pound while you fall!"

"Another Normal-type move?" Roxanne commented, surprised by such a risky choice. "Do you think you can defeat a mighty Pokémon like Geodude with attacks like that?"

But Ash had not acted randomly, and Roxanne soon understood his plan: by hitting Geodude at the same time as falling toward it, Treecko was able to give much more energy to the blow. It hit Geodude hard.

The power of the impact left everyone speechless, especially Roxanne. Unfortunately for Ash, however, Geodude recovered almost immediately. The Gym Leader had it use Rollout and then Mega Punch again, and this time Treecko couldn't fight back. The inexperienced Pokémon was clearly no match for Geodude.

Ash called Treecko back and comforted it.

"Thank you, Treecko," he said as the Pokémon went back into its Poké Ball. "You battled bravely. Now rest."

Although the first round of the battle was over, the young Trainer wasn't discouraged. He seemed more determined than ever to show everyone what he knew how to do.

"Pikachu, it's your turn!" Ash cried.

"*Pika, pika!*" replied Pikachu, its whiskers sizzling with excitement.

"You really want to use an Electric-type Pokémon in a Rock-type Gym?" asked Roxanne, surprised again. She knew that Ash had some kind of strategy in mind,

but she couldn't figure it out. "I think you might regret it," she added with a smile.

"Just wait until you see us on the battlefield," Ash replied. "Go on, Pikachu. Use Thunder!"

"*Pikaaaaa-chuuuuu!*" shouted the Mouse Pokémon, and it unleashed a powerful strike.

The move left Geodude unharmed, just as the Gym Leader had expected, but it had another effect: the boulders had been cleared away from most of the battlefield.

Roxanne didn't seem bothered at all. "You might not realize that you just gave Geodude more space to launch its attacks!" she said.

Roxanne then had Geodude charge with another Rollout, but something unexpected happened. Since the ground had been left smooth by Pikachu's Thunder, the Rock Pokémon skidded around and wasn't able to get the push it needed to roll at full speed against its opponent!

Taking advantage of this moment of weakness, Ash had Pikachu attack again. This time, he got the effect he'd hoped for: after being hit hard, Geodude could no longer keep battling.

"Yesss!" Vera, Max, and Brock cheered from the stands.

"Congratulations, Ash," Roxanne said with admiration. "Until today, I had never lost with Geodude against an Electric-type Pokémon. But now let's see what you do with this one."

"This one," it soon became clear, was Nosepass.

A Rock-type Pokémon like Geodude, Nosepass had a huge electromagnetic nose that it used to determine the exact position of its opponents without

using sight, which was one of its weaker senses. It was so massive and intimidating that Pikachu was already looking anxious about the difficult battle ahead.

Ash, however, had not lost faith that they could win. When did they ever lose?

"Let's end this one in a hurry," he said with determination. "Pikachu, use Iron Tail!"

Pikachu immediately charged up its tail with all the energy it could muster, then took a leap and hit Nosepass with a powerful blow. Perfectly executed!

However . . .

Nosepass spun but didn't fall. Ash had Pikachu use

Iron Tail again, but this time the Mouse Pokémon's tail lit up only for an instant before going out.

I can't use Iron Tail too many times in a row, Ash realized, concerned. *It seems that Pikachu needs to regain energy between one attack and the next!*

He needed a different strategy. And now Nosepass was counterattacking with a fearsome Rock Tomb. Pikachu found itself trapped in a rocky prison with no way to escape.

Nosepass was a truly dangerous opponent!

To help Pikachu free itself, Ash suggested it use Thunder—and it worked! The Mouse Pokémon was able to shatter the rock and return to the ground. However, it was now very tired. Fighting against such a powerful opponent had worn it out!

Ash realized that the only way to continue the battle was to tire out Nosepass as well. And the only way to do that was through speed, not strength.

"Pikachu, Quick Attack!" he shouted. "Make it spin in circles!"

Pikachu began to run around Nosepass. The Compass Pokémon tried to catch Pikachu, but was too big and slow for the quick Mouse Pokémon. Nosepass's poor vision made things even worse, since it was hard to follow the little yellow flash rushing around it at full speed.

Roxanne knew that her Pokémon was getting tired and disoriented. She decided to change tactics.

"Nosepass, you can't find Pikachu with your eyes," she called. "Use your nose to locate its electric charge!"

Before Nosepass could follow its Trainer's instructions, Ash asked Pikachu to use Iron Tail. The battle needed to end!

But once again, the move wasn't enough. Pikachu still hadn't recharged its energy reserve!

Roxanne took the opportunity to have Nosepass attack with Thunder Wave, which hit the Mouse Pokémon and drained its strength.

By now, Ash's hope of victory was almost gone. Pikachu was panting, a sign that it could only fight a little longer.

"Do you think you can go on, Pikachu?" he asked.

"*Pika!*" it replied, determined not to give in.

Ash smiled at this and, noticing Roxanne's surprise, explained, "The more difficult the battle, the more determined Pikachu and I are to pull out all the stops."

Roxanne grinned—then told Nosepass to use Zap Cannon, an Electric-type move.

At that point, Ash had a daring idea. It could work, as long as Roxanne didn't realize what he was going to do.

"Don't react, Pikachu!" he shouted.

Pikachu obeyed without a moment's hesitation, and Nosepass's move hit it full force.

Vera, Max, and Brock each held their breath as they watched the scene unfold. Why had their friend given that instruction? How could Pikachu, already so weakened, withstand such a powerful move?

The answer was soon revealed.

Not only did Nosepass's attack fail to knock out Pikachu, it had the exact opposite effect! The flow of energy from the Zap Cannon recharged Pikachu's electricity reserves—and now it could launch a powerful counterattack.

Nosepass was nearly paralyzed by the effect of Pikachu's electric shock, and then Ash ordered up another Iron Tail.

This time, the move was effective, because Pikachu was at full power!

Nosepass couldn't avoid the attack, and fell backward heavily. Ash and Pikachu had defeated it using its own powers against it!

Roxanne was flabbergasted. Her opponents were so in tune with each other that they were able to overcome even being at a great disadvantage. The Trainer's intelligence, along with the Pokémon's perseverance, had resulted in an incredibly exciting battle.

"I've never seen a team as close as you two," the Gym Leader said, admitting defeat. "Thank you for the excellent battle. I am truly happy to award you the Stone Badge."

"Thank you!" Ash replied. He received the badge with pride. "We learned a lot fighting in your Gym, Roxanne, and now we're ready for new challenges! Right, Pikachu?"

"*Pikaaa!*" the Pokémon confirmed. Ash and his partner were always on the same page!

ZOOM IN ON . . .

Whoever finds a friend finds a treasure—and Ash has struck gold! During his adventures he meets many new friends who help him become a Trainer and a better person.

MISTY

Misty dreams of becoming the best Trainer of Water-type Pokémon, and that's why she sets out on adventures with Ash. She's thoughtful but also fierce, and she always tries her hardest.

BROCK

Taking care of others is in Brock's DNA. He also loves learning and understanding many points of view. His only weakness is for girls: he always loses his head over them!

MAY AND MAX

May's dream is to see the world, and little by little she's finding her calling as a Pokémon Coordinator. Her brother Max also wants to travel—but through reading. May and Max are as different as cats and dogs, but they love each other dearly.

IRIS

Iris's destiny is to become a Dragon Master. She's like a big sister to Ash, and often scolds him gently. But they actually have a lot in common, including a strong sense of determination.

MANY FRIENDS, MANY ADVENTURES

CILAN

As a Gym Leader and Pokémon Expert, Cilan is an ideal travel companion for Ash because they complement each other: While Ash is impulsive and sometimes too hasty, Cilan is always calm and careful. Plus, he's an excellent cook!

CLEMONT AND BONNIE

Clemont is a genuine genius, capable of building machines for any type of situation (although they don't always work!). His biggest fan is his sister, Bonnie, a sweet but cheeky little girl.

SERENA

Serena and Ash met when they were little kids, and at the time, Ash said to her, "Never give up until the end." Ever since then, they've supported each other in making their dreams come true.

KIAWE

Kiawe has the spirit of a true warrior. In spite of his fierce appearance, he has a good heart and is a true friend to Ash. He has a little sister, Mimo, and he's a big softie with her!

GOH

Goh's goal is to catch every Pokémon he meets, and not let anything stop him. He greatly admires Ash and is always ready to lend him a hand.

SINNOH

THE STRENGTH OF FRIENDSHIP

"What an epic battle!" the voice from the loudspeaker squawked. "Ash and Paul, along with their Pokémon, just demonstrated their incredible capabilities."

Cheers of excitement from the crowd in the stands drowned out every other noise.

That sunny afternoon, Ash was in a full, six-on-six battle against his rival Paul from Veilstone City. They were competing in the quarterfinals of the Sinnoh League championship on Lily of the Valley Island, and both Trainers were very determined to win and move forward.

Ash and Paul already knew each other. While traveling throughout Sinnoh, Ash had met this intense boy many times, and had even battled against him a few times. But they had never become friends. They were too different!

Ash was easygoing and sociable, and had built a close bond with his Pokémon. Paul, on the other hand, always seemed unhappy, and was focused solely on winning. If his Pokémon didn't show the highest levels of skill, he often abandoned them.

In spite of these differences, the two boys had something in common: a firm determination to improve. Even when in a tough battle, they always tried to learn from the strategies used by their opponents.

And so, each time they met, Ash and Paul studied each other and absorbed new ideas. Their healthy rivalry helped each of them grow.

Now, for the first time, they were facing off against each other on an official battlefield, in front of thousands

of spectators. For the moment, the fight was going Ash's way.

At that point, Paul had gone through five of his Pokémon, but Ash had two left: Pikachu and Infernape. Both had already taken some damage, though, because Ash had already sent them out onto the battlefield and then called them back while they still had energy.

So the fate of the battle was not yet set in stone.

Paul called on his Electivire, which had defeated Ash's Gliscor despite being at a type disadvantage. Now it would face Pikachu in a clash of Electric types.

As soon as the Mouse Pokémon stepped forward, Paul gave Electivire its first command: "Use Thunder on the battlefield!"

Electivire followed his instructions, placing its hands and the tips of its two tails on the ground. That transferred the move's energy into the ground, breaking it up and throwing heavy clods of dirt into the air. Paul's intent was to hit Pikachu with the dirt, as he'd done with Ash's Gliscor, but this time Ash knew what to expect.

"Pikachu, Quick Attack!" he shouted.

The Pokémon immediately understood its Trainer's plan. Using the speed of the move to avoid the dirt clods, it jumped onto one of them in midair and launched itself toward its opponent.

"Pikachu's Quick Attack hit Electivire right in the face!" the announcer commented.

Paul wasted no time in ordering his Pokémon to block Pikachu, trapping it with its two tails.

But Ash didn't seem bothered, which Paul noticed. "I have a feeling you were expecting that move," he spat. "Unfortunately for you, Pikachu has already suffered a lot of damage, while Electivire is in perfect shape."

"Pikachu is just fine," replied Ash. Then he added, "Pikachu, use Iron Tail to free yourself!"

Paul smiled. Pikachu was too small compared to Electivire. It would need a terrifying amount of energy to escape those powerful tails. However, to his great surprise, Pikachu managed to break through. "It's much stronger than I expected!" Paul murmured, gritting his teeth. After a quick calculation, the boy gave his next command. "Quick, Electivire, use Brick Break!"

"Block it with a Quick Attack!" shouted Ash.

The two Pokémon met in the center of the battlefield, emitting such a powerful glow that it covered both Trainers and even the crowd in the stands.

They're in a stalemate, thought Paul, watching the scene unfold. *This isn't just about Trainers and talent. Pikachu has something more, otherwise there's no explanation for how it could defend itself against Electivire given all the hits it's taken in the other fights. Maybe there really is some special power in the bond between this Pokémon and Ash.*

Paul tried to shake this thought. He had always been

convinced that the secret to success lay in discipline and hard work, and he demanded the best from his Pokémon. He loved his Pokémon, but at the same time he didn't want to let sentiment get in the way of his goals—he was sure that being the best required being cold-blooded, with no unnecessary gestures of affection.

Since he'd met Ash, though, there had been a crack in his theory. And now it seemed on the verge of disintegrating, seeing Pikachu's determination as it launched an attack with Volt Tackle.

This was no time to get distracted. He needed to react.

"An Electric-type move?" asked Paul, pretending to be confident. "That won't have any effect on Electivire. Block it, quick!"

Electivire stretched out its hands and used Motor Drive, a special ability that allowed it to cancel out the effects of an Electric-type move and increase its own speed at the same time. Repelling Pikachu, the Thunderbolt Pokémon fought back with a stronger Thunder Punch than ever.

"Just as I thought!" cried Ash. "Go on, Pikachu, use Iron Tail!"

Pikachu took a leap and managed to strike Electivire before being struck itself.

But it wasn't enough. The two Pokémon were stuck in a deadlock, and neither was able to overcome the other. Now it was Ash's turn to wonder about the likelihood of victory. Up until that moment, he had no doubt that he could defeat Paul. He'd hoped that Pikachu's Iron Tail would be enough to knock out Electivire.

But . . .

"Don't you remember?" Paul said. "This is the same situation we were in the first time we battled. You wanted to close out the match with Iron Tail, but now Pikachu has been blocked—and as soon as it moves again, it will be overpowered by the Thunder Punch. And there's another move that Electivire can perform with just its left arm: BRICK BREAK!"

At that, Electivire hit Pikachu with a powerful blow and sent it flying.

The Mouse Pokémon tried to get up one last time, but its strength was gone. It fell to the ground. The battle was definitely over for Pikachu.

Ash ran to take his partner in his arms. He brought it to a quiet corner where it could recover.

"Thank you, my friend," he said tenderly. "You did your best, as always. I promise we'll win for you!"

Those words struck Paul more than he had expected. Pikachu wasn't fighting *for* Ash, but *with* Ash. Their feelings and their wishes were in perfect harmony. That's why Ash and his Pokémon were so strong together.

Paul's theory was confirmed when Ash brought out his final Pokémon, Infernape. Like Pikachu, it had already taken damage in the earlier stages of the battle, but it took the field without hesitation.

A full-on battle between Infernape and Electivire began, making the stadium shake. In the end, with a brutal sequence of Flamethrower, Mach Punch, and Flare Blitz, Infernape got the better of Electivire.

Ash had won!

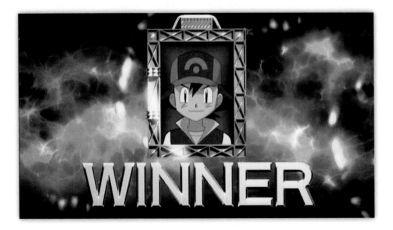

Only at that point did Infernape begin to show how weak it was from the difficult battle—but Ash rushed over to support his Pokémon before it fell.

Meanwhile, Paul kneeled next to his defeated Electivire to put it back in its Poké Ball. He said to it, "Thank you. You were truly great."

It was the first time Paul had thanked any of his Pokémon, especially when they'd lost, and it felt a little strange. But he had decided that from that moment on, his Training methods would change, and he would allow more room for emotion.

Ash's example had helped him understand the real secret to a strong Pokémon: true, devoted friendship.

UNOVA

5

LET'S SAVE
UNOVA!

An enormous gray helicopter appeared on the horizon over the sea. The noisy aircraft approached a floating platform, then landed. A hatch opened and a man in a gray jumpsuit stepped out. Waiting for him on the platform was a small army standing at attention, as well as Jessie, James, and Meowth.

The man looked around with a sneer, inspecting his troops, who were awaiting orders.

"Today is the day the Unova region will fall into the hands of Team Rocket," he declared with great satisfaction. "The final phase of Operation Tempest starts now!"

Nearby, in the gardens of a beautiful villa in Undella Town, Ash was busy with some special training alongside his friends Iris and Cilan. They were all guests of the Champion Cynthia.

Ash had every intention of participating in the upcoming Unova League, and winning!

At that moment, his Oshawott was battling against Cilan's Pansage. Oshawott was performing really well, especially because it wanted to impress Meloetta, a beautiful Pokémon that had been traveling with them. Ash had saved Meloetta's life in a truly dramatic moment after it had been chased by villains who wanted to catch it.

Now, however, that terrible time in Meloetta's life was just a memory. The garden of this beautiful house was peaceful and serene, and Meloetta enjoyed watching training. In fact, for the first time since it had joined the group, the Pokémon seemed to want to participate, too.

To everyone's surprise, Meloetta whirled onto the battlefield to face off against Oshawott and then did something unexpected: it began to sing.

Ash and his friends were enchanted by the sound. Meloetta had a wonderful, moving voice, and for its entire performance both the humans and the Pokémon didn't dare move a muscle. Especially not Oshawott, who had a crush on Meloetta!

Meloetta wasn't singing just for fun, though. The melody allowed it to change into its Pirouette Forme. By singing and dancing, Meloetta transformed right before them: its eyes and hair changed from green to vibrant orange, and its hair took on a new shape.

But none of the friends could have imagined that, hiding amid the tree branches, there was a small electronic device that looked like a spider with a single eye. It was sent there for one, evil purpose: to record the sweet song of the Melody Pokémon.

Ignorant of how close its enemies were, Meloetta was ready to show off what it could do. Oshawott, however, was torn. It didn't want to fight against such a sweet creature!

"You can do it!" Ash encouraged Oshawott, seeing its hesitation. "We're just training."

But the Sea Otter Pokémon shook its head no several times, and Ash knew not to insist.

"Very well." He sighed. "Krookodile, you're up!"

Krookodile didn't need to be asked twice—but before it could take a single step, it was hit by Meloetta's Hyper Voice.

Though the move was powerful, Krookodile managed to resist, then counterattacked with Stone Edge. But Meloetta sent the stones right back with Close Combat.

"Fantastic! Meloetta is perfect for this kind of training!" Ash cheered. He was having a great time, as were the rest of his friends.

But their fun was soon interrupted. Krookodile was about to launch its next move when a rumble came from the sky, quickly followed by a dazzling burst of flame. A huge creature landed in front of them: Golurk, the Automaton Pokémon, a giant whose footsteps made the earth shake.

"What's going on?" Ash cried. Pikachu bravely stepped in front of him, ready to defend him against this potential threat.

Suddenly, they realized there was someone on Golurk's shoulder! It was a young man wearing aviator goggles. He jumped down and ran toward Meloetta so quickly that no one was able to react, except Meloetta. As soon as Meloetta saw the boy, it ran to embrace him.

"Are you okay, Meloetta? Is everything all right?" the boy asked, hugging the Pokémon tightly. Clearly they knew each other well.

Surprised, Ash walked over and started to say something. But the boy gave him a fiery look and cried, "You scoundrel! You stole Meloetta!"

"I . . . what?" asked Ash, even more surprised. He didn't have a chance to try to explain what had happened before the newcomer called, "Golurk, use Flash Cannon!"

At this command, the big Pokémon raised a hand and turned toward Ash, who was frozen in shock. Pikachu's whiskers sizzled, waiting for Ash to give it instructions for a counterattack. But before the situation could escalate, Meloetta rushed to stand between Ash and Golurk, stopping the big Pokémon from striking. The Automaton Pokémon pulled back and stopped preparing its attack.

"Meloetta!" the boy cried. "Why did you defend him?"

"I am not a thief," Ash finally said. "And I think you owe us an explanation."

"*Pika, pika!*" Pikachu agreed.

The boy looked into Meloetta's eyes and saw genuine concern, so he realized he had made a mistake.

"Forgive me, I jumped to conclusions," he said, turning to Ash. "You're right, I'll explain everything to you."

Iris came over. "I think we all need to calm down," she said. "Let's go sit and talk over a cup of tea, shall we?"

Soon they were all seated in the elegant drawing room. Meloetta was back to its Aria Forme, and the boy began to tell his story.

"My name is Ridley," he said. "Golurk and I have been searching for Meloetta for a long time. The three of us were living hidden in a forest in the Unova region, until one day we were discovered. While I was away, villains came and kidnapped Meloetta. They knew about

Meloetta's immense power and wanted to take it for themselves. I was far away at the time, but there's a deep connection between Meloetta and me, and I felt its cries for help. Unfortunately, by the time I got back, it was too late: Meloetta was caught in a trap. I called on Golurk for help, but the kidnappers used Yamask to create a thick blanket of smoke that stopped us. We couldn't attack anyone in the dark cloud without the risk of injuring Meloetta! When we managed to fly beyond the smoke, the kidnappers' helicopter had already disappeared. And it was all my fault. I shouldn't have left Meloetta alone for even a moment."

Ridley sighed. Clearly this memory was very painful for him. Meloetta flew over and hugged him.

"From that moment on, I've been searching nonstop," Ridley continued. "I could feel Meloetta's emotions, but I didn't have any way to track it. Then, a little while

ago, I finally heard its song, which guided me here. I assumed you must have been involved in Meloetta's disappearance, and that's why I attacked you. I beg your forgiveness."

"Don't worry, it's water under the bridge," Iris said with a smile. "So Meloetta is one of your Pokémon?"

"No," Ridley replied. "Meloetta doesn't belong to anyone! It's a Mythical Pokémon from Unova, and there are many legends about it. Since ancient times, people called Protectors have had the responsibility of keeping it safe. I am one of them. Unfortunately I failed. I'm sure that those criminals are already on our trail. I must take Meloetta away before they find us!"

Meloetta, meanwhile, was twirling around the room. In spite of the obvious dangers Ridley had recounted, Meloetta seemed calm. There, with its Protector and its new friends, it felt completely safe.

Then it saw something.

A drone was buzzing outside the window with its camera pointed at the house!

The Mythical Pokémon let out a shriek and Ridley rushed to its side.

"Oh no!" he cried, seeing the drone. "They're already here! We've got to escape! Meloetta, come on!"

"Where do you think you'll go?" asked Ash, worried. "By now they know about your hiding place in the forest."

"My friends have already found a safe place for us," Ridley replied while running out of the house, where Golurk was waiting for them.

But it was too late. A troublesome cloud of smoke from a Yamask surrounded them, signaling that the attack had already begun. Ridley climbed up onto Golurk's shoulders with Meloetta in his arms, but something hit the big Pokémon with the power of a cannonball. Meloetta was thrown to the ground.

The object that had hit them turned out to be a Golem, and a few moments later a Rhydon appeared, ready to attack. Then two people in uniforms with an "R" printed on the chest emerged from the smoke.

"That's enough!" shouted Ridley, putting up his fists. "Who are you?"

"They're from Team Rocket," Ash said. He recognized the uniforms. "They steal Pokémon for their own evil purposes."

Cilan added, "We've fought Team Rocket many times."

The two criminals wasted no time introducing themselves and went straight into battle mode.

"Rhydon, Megahorn!" one of them commanded.

"Golurk, use Strength!" Ridley shouted.

"Go, Golem, Rock Blast!" shrieked the second assailant.

Through the blasts and the dense smoke that surrounded them, Ash and the others had a hard time knowing how the battle was really going. But they all had the same priority.

"Take Meloetta to safety!" shouted Ridley. "I'll take care of Team Rocket."

Ash knew the Mythical Pokémon shouldn't stay there a moment longer. So while Golurk fought bravely against their enemies, Ash, Iris, and Cilan led Meloetta toward the woods that surrounded the house.

"Meloetta, you should turn yourself invisible!" Cilan suggested.

It nodded and its body dissolved, disappearing from sight.

But their escape was soon blocked by a circle of Will-O-Wisp, shortly followed by three familiar faces: Jessie, James, and Meowth!

"You again?!" shouted Ash.

James ordered Yamask to strike them again with Will-O-Wisp—and pointed out for his Pokémon exactly where Meloetta was. The move hit Meloetta with full force, making it turn visible again. James, Jessie, and

Meowth were wearing special glasses that gave them the power to see things that were invisible!

"What do you want?" Iris burst out.

"It would take too long to explain," James replied with a wicked grin.

"In any case, we should be thanking you for inspiring Meloetta to sing," added Jessie.

"What are you talking about?" asked Ash, more irritated than ever.

"Hand over Meloetta and no one gets hurt," was their only reply.

"Not a chance!" Ash replied. "Pikachu, use Thunderbolt!"

Pikachu launched the attack. "*Pikaaa!*"

"Dodge it and use Air Slash!" Jessie commanded Woobat, which did so.

"Yamask, use Haze!" shouted James.

"Go on, Axew," Iris cried. "Dragon Rage!"

"Pansage, it's time to use Bullet Seed!" said Cilan.

A flurry of strikes followed. Cilan took advantage of the confusion to tell Ash to escape. "Take Meloetta— we'll cover you!"

Ash knew that it was the right thing to do. Even though he hated to leave his friends in danger, he quickly made his way into the woods with the Mythical Pokémon.

He had taken only a few steps when Pikachu suddenly stopped. It had heard something.

"What's up, Pikachu?" Ash asked, his heart pounding.

Just then, a Persian jumped out of a bush with an evil growl.

"Make yourself invisible, quick," Ash whispered to Meloetta, who immediately disappeared. Persian stared at them with eyes as cold as rubies, ready to spring.

With Meloetta hidden, Ash was about to have Pikachu attack when Giovanni, the evil leader of Team Rocket, appeared from the thick foliage! He was wearing glasses just like James's and Jessie's, and looked around smugly.

"Meloetta, I know you're here," he said with a sneer. "Persian, use Shadow Claw!"

Persian followed his command, and Ash had Pikachu try to counterattack with Iron Tail. It stopped Giovanni's Pokémon for only an instant, and Ash and Pikachu were soon overwhelmed by a Power Gem that threw them to the ground. Seeing its friends hit so hard, Meloetta rushed over to make sure they were okay.

Giovanni was just waiting for that to happen.

From a helicopter above, a beam of light shot down and then closed around Ash and Pikachu in a cage, trapping them.

"Meloetta," said Giovanni, "do as I say, or your friends will have a messy end. I can crush them to pieces in a matter of seconds!"

At that, the force field began to close in around Ash and Pikachu, as if to crush them. No matter what they tried, they couldn't free themselves!

"Quick, Meloetta! Escape!" shouted Ash.

But Meloetta couldn't move for fear that Giovanni might follow through on his evil threat. And so a force field cage surrounded Meloetta as well, and both it and Ash and Pikachu were pulled up to the helicopter.

When Iris and Cilan arrived a few moments later, there was nothing they could do but watch helplessly as their friends were put inside the aircraft and taken away.

The helicopter flew over the woods to the sea, where Team Rocket took the prisoners aboard a submarine. It silently sank beneath the surface of the water and into the deep. Two headlights lit its path through the darkness, revealing what looked like a large underwater mountain.

But it wasn't a mountain. According to legend, deep in the sea near Unova there was an underwater temple that contained a great secret. No one had set foot there for many, many years, but Team Rocket had found it—and now they were taking Meloetta there for what they called "Operation Tempest."

The submarine glided through a stone tunnel and down a long corridor lined with columns, finally emerging in a gigantic chamber with a very high ceiling.

The water came only to the floor of the chamber. Giovanni got out of the submarine along with Jessie, James, and Meowth, as well as Dr. Zager, Team Rocket's crooked scientist.

The group stood on a large, circular platform in the middle of the water. A door on the submarine opened and released the cages that still imprisoned Ash, Pikachu, and Meloetta, which floated up into the air in the center of the chamber.

"You recognize this place, don't you, Meloetta?" Giovanni sneered.

"What are you planning to do?" Ash shouted.

"Be quiet and you'll see," Giovanni replied.

The cube that contained Meloetta flew higher until it was positioned next to a stone slab floating in the air. The slab had a shape cut out of the center of it. At Dr. Zager's command, the force field cage around the Mythical Pokémon dissolved and it was immediately imprisoned in the cut-out stone.

"Listen carefully, Meloetta," Giovanni continued. "You must not resist, or the boy and his friend will pay dearly."

James added, "Normally the ceremony would require you to sing to unlock the seal, but this time there is no need"

"What seal?" shouted Ash, beating his fists against the translucent cube.

No one from Team Rocket paid attention to him. Meowth shot him a scornful look, then pushed a button. Meloetta's voice, which had been recorded a few hours earlier, filled the temple.

At the first notes of that song, the entire building started to tremble. The chamber floor began to move, spinning upward to form a tall pyramid.

Giovanni began to climb a spiral staircase that encircled the pyramid, ascending slowly to savor his triumph.

"Meloetta," the man said, "living with this boy and his friends has brought peace to your heart, and this is what made it possible for you to sing your song again. Only this long-lost song has the power to open the seal. It wouldn't have worked if you had been found in a state of anger or fear: This is why we've been following you and waited until you sang on your own."

While Giovanni spoke, a mirror on a stone pedestal emerged from the pyramid's peak. Giovanni stood before it and cheered, "Here it is! The Reveal Glass!"

Meloetta's eyes had started glowing with white light.

Giovanni cried, "Great temple! Listen to our voices, emerge from the sea, and summon the three great powers!"

These words triggered an earthquake, and the underwater temple detached from the sea floor and began to rise to the surface.

Soon the temple stood above the waves in all its glory, surrounded by a maze of stones.

The water had just stopped flowing off the building when the pyramid's peak opened, revealing Giovanni and his prisoners. The stone slab containing Meloetta was still floating in midair. By now, Meloetta was completely incapable of stopping what was happening.

As it was created to do, the Reveal Glass absorbed Meloetta's power and rose up off its pedestal. When the sunlight hit it, a dazzling beam of light burst forth from the smooth surface and tore through the sky.

That ray of light was visible at such a great distance that Ridley, Iris, Cilan, and Cynthia noticed it from their speedboat. They were scouring the ocean in the hopes of saving their friends.

"They did it!" Ridley cried, full of rage. "We must act quickly!"

"What is that beam of light?" asked Iris, unable to look away from the sky.

"It's the signal that Team Rocket has completed the ritual," Ridley replied. "Through Meloetta, they are calling forth the three Legendary Pokémon of Unova to control the forces of nature. Generation after generation, the only ones to have this power have been the Protectors who lived alongside Meloetta. But there were always people who wanted to use these forces for evil, and so, long ago, Meloetta decided to sink the temple into the sea and disappear from history along with my ancestors."

As Ridley spoke, the sky was quickly filling with a heavy blanket of dark clouds. Taller and taller waves crashed against the boat, which was speeding toward the temple.

Then, amid thunder and lightning, the three Legendary Pokémon of Unova appeared through the clouds: Tornadus, Thundurus, and Landorus.

Ash witnessed their arrival and knew there was very little time to act. No one was paying attention to him, so it was the perfect moment to try to escape.

"Pikachu," he said, "use Iron Tail to break this cage. Concentrate your strength on a single point!"

Pikachu summoned all its energy, and after a series of formidable strikes, managed to break the barrier. As

soon as they were free, the pair ran toward Meloetta, but they were immediately stopped by Woobat and Yamask with a cross attack that flung them off the temple wall.

Ash and Pikachu would have ended up in the sea if Golurk hadn't arrived just in time to stop their fall. The Automaton Pokémon grabbed them in its big arms, then took them to Ridley and the others, who had just arrived at the artificial island.

"Thanks, Golurk!" said Ash as he jumped to the ground.

"Are you okay?" asked Iris, running to hug them.

"Yeah," replied Ash. "But Meloetta is in danger and Team Rocket has summoned the three Legendary Pokémon. We must stop them at all costs!"

"There's not a moment to waste!" cried Cynthia, tossing a Poké Ball. "Garchomp, go!"

Iris and Cilan followed her example and called forth Dragonite and Pansage.

"Unfezant, I choose you!" Ash said,

bringing out the Proud Pokémon. Then he turned to Pikachu and added, "I need your help, too!"

Pikachu nodded. It jumped onto Unfezant's shoulder, and they joined their companions to go free Meloetta.

Meanwhile, using the power of the Reveal Glass, Giovanni had tricked the Legendary Pokémon into assuming their Therian Formes. Tornadus was winged with green feathers, Thunderus became dragon-like, and Landorus changed into a Pokémon that walked on four paws.

Once the transformation was complete, the Reveal Glass descended back onto the pedestal as Giovanni let out an evil cackle. For a moment, his eyes turned red and glassy, but no one noticed.

"Forces of Nature, hear me!" Giovanni declared. "Now you are at my command! Use the powers of wind, thunder, and earth to give me control over Unova!"

To his great disappointment, however, the Legendary Pokémon had more pressing matters to deal with first: an attack from Pikachu, Dragonite, and their friends! Ash's and his friends' Pokémon were launching an attack all at the same time!

"Listen to me," Giovanni called to the Legendary Pokémon. "You must stop anyone who dares to get in your way!"

But the Legendary trio was already attacking the other Pokémon mercilessly.

Dragonite was first. It was hit with Air Slash and Stone Edge from Tornadus and Landorus. After Dragonite fell to the ground, Thundurus hurled an electric shock at it. Iris rushed to try to shield her Pokémon with her own body. It was an action she made purely on instinct, not considering that there was no hope of protecting her Pokémon—and that she might pay for her action with her life!

Luckily, Pikachu was faster. It arrived on Unfezant's wings and launched itself between Iris and Thundurus. The Electric-type Pokémon's little body completely absorbed the energy unleashed by the Legendary Pokémon.

"Pikachu!" shouted Ash, gathering it up in his

arms before it could fall to the ground. "You did an extraordinarily brave thing!"

"I don't know how to thank you, Pikachu!" Iris said, still gasping for breath.

"*Pika, pika,*" the Mouse Pokémon replied with a smile.

But there was no time to linger: Meloetta was still in danger and Team Rocket's mission was almost complete.

Dragonite struggled back to its feet, let out a deep roar, and then bolted up to rejoin the battle. Meanwhile, Ash began to climb the steps to the top of the temple with Pikachu and Unfezant.

The battle, high up in the sky, continued more bitterly than ever. There were only three Legendary Pokémon, but their moves had exceptional power. Dragonite and the others tried to fight against them, but they seemed unstoppable.

Then Giovanni, still standing in front of the Reveal Glass, stretched out his arms and shouted, "I order you to unleash your true power!"

At that, Meloetta gave out a terrible cry. The light in its eyes turned red, as did the eyes of Tornadus, Thundurus, and Landorus. Then the three Forces of Nature launched a final, decisive attack.

Most of the Pokémon fighting them were hurled away like leaves in a storm and crashed into the sea. Only

Pikachu and Unfezant remained unharmed, because they were still climbing the temple steps. But what could they alone do against these powerful creatures?

The Legendary Pokémon, still controlled by Giovanni, turned their powers to the water surrounding the temple. They had soon transformed the sea into an immense icy plain.

The ice then spread onto dry land, invading the countryside and reaching all the way to cities. People fled in fear, unable to understand what was happening.

The power of the Legendary Pokémon shocked even Jessie, James, Meowth, and Dr. Zager, who watched the world transform into a land of ice. They thought that victory surely must be close at hand—but they were wrong!

Dragonite, Golurk, Garchomp, and Pansage burst through the ice over the sea and took their battle positions, just as Ash reached the top of the pyramid with Pikachu and Unfezant.

"Too late, boy," Jessie cried. "You can't stop us!"

"It's not going to end like this!" Ash replied. "Meloetta is coming with me! Pikachu, Electro Ball!"

Team Rocket watched in shock as Pikachu leaped up and formed a mass of electricity around its body that got bigger and bigger. Soon the Electro Ball was enormous, illuminating the sea all around it. Then Pikachu hurled it at the pyramid with the power of a meteor—causing the temple to collapse.

BOOOOOM!

The energy released from Pikachu's attack was so intense that it freed Meloetta from its prison in the stone slab. But the Mythical Pokémon was still unconscious and in danger of falling—until, with lightning-quick reflexes, Ash sent Unfezant to save it!

A column of dust and debris rose up from the temple. Where Giovanni and the Reveal Glass once stood was now just a ruin.

Meloetta woke up and Unfezant brought it to Ash. He greeted it with a hug.

"You're safe!" the boy cried, relieved.

Meloetta smiled—then turned radiant upon seeing Ridley running toward them.

Meanwhile, James shouted, "Meloetta escaped!"

"Let's go get it!" said Meowth.

"I don't . . . need Meloetta . . . anymore," Giovanni said in a raspy voice. He was sprawled on the ground, and slowly lifted himself up. His face was terrifying! A strange red, circular symbol had appeared on his forehead, and his eyes glowed red. "I feel all-powerful!" he said. "I am ready for DESTRUCTION!"

"Destruction? What do you mean?" asked Jessie, confused and concerned about their leader's transformation.

"That's not the plan," said James. "Our goal is to *conquer* Unova, not destroy it!"

Giovanni completely ignored their protests. The power that he'd invoked had overwhelmed him and now controlled him.

"NO ONE CAN STOP ME!" Giovanni shouted, his face twisted.

"What's wrong with him?" asked Meowth.

It was Ridley, nearby on the pyramid, who replied. "The three Legendary Pokémon possess the unlimited power of nature," he explained. "But it's Meloetta that maintains the sanity of whoever summons them. Now that he doesn't have Meloetta, that man has been completely consumed by his evil ambitions. That's why his goal is simply to sow chaos."

Giovanni seemed completely indifferent to what was happening around him. With his arms spread wide and his eyes fixed on the Forces of Nature, he seemed focused only on the goal of total destruction.

With his mind, Giovanni commanded Tornadus, Thundurus, and Landorus to fight back against Golurk and the others—his final obstacles to overcome.

As everyone saw what was about to take place, Meowth cried, "We won't let that happen!"

"We must save the boss!" shouted Jessie.

The trio from Team Rocket launched themselves at Giovanni and dragged him away from the area where the temple's power was focused. They had the right instinct: once they were far away from the Reveal Glass, Giovanni regained his senses and the fiery symbol disappeared from his forehead.

"What's going on?" he asked, confused and in shock. He got to his feet with the help of Jessie and James.

"We lost Meloetta and we can't control the Legendary Pokémon," replied Dr. Zager. "I'm afraid we have no choice but to retreat."

Giovanni looked up toward Ash and his friends and knew that Zager was right. He begrudgingly admitted defeat.

In spite of it all, he felt relieved. He still felt the enormity of the power that had controlled him, and now knew how dangerous it was. He was at the point of destroying the entire region of Unova. And then what good would it be to rule over it?

"Very well, let's retreat!" he said.

"Yessir!" replied Jessie, James, and Meowth.

Supported by his henchmen, Giovanni reached their helicopter. Jessie and James took control, and the aircraft took off while Yamask covered their tracks with a cloud of gas.

Ash and the others couldn't stop them—and there were more urgent problems to deal with.

The three Legendary Pokémon were still free, and still fighting against Dragonite, Golurk, Garchomp, and Pansage. The sky was lit up by the flurry of strikes. By now, the Forces of Nature had been fully unleashed and were ready to carry out destruction.

Luckily, Ridley knew just what to do! He recovered the Reveal Glass and placed it back on its stone pedestal.

"We need to stop them!" he said to Meloetta. While Meloetta flew up above the temple, Ridley looked at the image reflected in the mirror and said, "I beg you, hear my wish. Calm the rage that threatens Unova!"

The Reveal Glass obeyed: beams of iridescent light shot out from it and whirled up to Meloetta.

Infused with this energy, the Mythical Pokémon began to sing with its beautiful voice. An enchanting melody spread through the air like a gentle wind and drew the Forces of Nature over to Meloetta. The extraordinary song reached their hardened hearts and freed them from their rage.

A few moments later, Tornadus, Thundurus, and Landorus each returned to their Incarnate Forme, and were at peace at last.

The ice melted. The sea once again formed gentle waves beneath a clear sky.

The Forces of Nature could now return to their realm to rest.

Ash and his companions boarded the speedboat to head for shore.

Behind them, the temple once again slowly sank into the sea, as Meloetta had wanted long ago, and peace returned to the Unova region.

"I can't believe that Team Rocket orchestrated such an evil plan," Ash commented, watching the building disappear beneath the waves.

"It seems that conflict will never end," said Ridley. "There are always people who wish for power and will do anything to get it."

"But there are also people who fight for good," added Cynthia. "Not all are motivated by the desire to rule over others."

Ash and Pikachu shared a knowing look. They knew they would always fight to maintain peace, together.

The world of Pokémon is rich with variety. In addition to all the different kinds of Pokémon, many can evolve or assume different forms!

EVOLUTION

The majority of Pokémon go through several evolutionary states, which generally allow them to become more powerful and learn new moves. Some Pokémon may also decide not to evolve. For example, Pikachu prefers to become stronger staying just as it is, training with Ash.

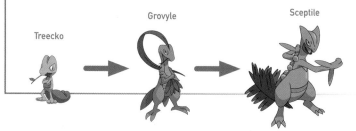

Treecko   Grovyle   Sceptile

FORMS

Some Pokémon can assume different forms without evolving. In some cases, a Pokémon can change appearance permanently depending on the environment in which it lives. Other times, Pokémon can change form temporarily, like Meloetta, who can change from its Aria Forme to the Pirouette Forme and vice versa in just moments. Some Pokémon look very different in their alternate forms: Zygarde, for example, is capable of truly spectacular metamorphoses!

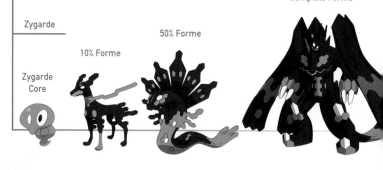

Zygarde

Zygarde Core   10% Forme   50% Forme   Complete Forme

CHANGES

MEGA EVOLUTIONS

Some Pokémon can Mega Evolve, as long as they are in possession of a Mega Stone and a Trainer with a Key Stone (two objects unique to each Pokémon). Only Trainers and Pokémon with a deep bond can use them. Mega Evolution is temporary and typically stops at the end of a battle.

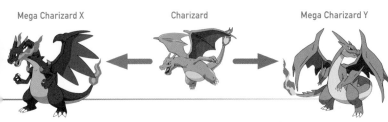

Mega Charizard X   Charizard   Mega Charizard Y

PRIMAL REVERSION

Like Mega Evolution, Primal Reversion is a temporary change in appearance and in the power of a Pokémon. In order for the Primal Reversion to happen, the Pokémon must have a special Sphere and draw on the power of nature.

Kyogre   Primal Kyogre

DYNAMAX AND GIGANTAMAX

Some Pokémon are able to assume a Dynamax or Gigantamax form, becoming enormous and gaining the capability of using very powerful moves. To activate the transformation, the Trainer must possess a special Dynamax Band. Unlike a Dynamax, a Gigantamax Pokémon changes its appearance in addition to increasing in size.

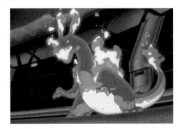

TAKE CARE OF IT, PIKACHU!

There's a special place in the Kalos region, a place everyone who loves Pokémon dreams of visiting at least once: the factory where Poké Balls are made!

Ash and Pikachu were traveling toward Anistar City with Clemont, Bonnie, and Serena. They couldn't pass up the chance to take a peek at such a fascinating site, even though they weren't sure they'd be able to get permission to enter.

Clemont was particularly eager. He loved technology, and was very interested to see the machines at work creating those ingenious spheres. He was even excited just to be near such a majestic building.

The group was greeted by a man and two women, who introduced themselves as the deputy director, director, and secretary.

"We are delighted to receive guests, and we would be happy to give you a special tour of the factory," the director said. "Follow us!"

The friends hadn't expected such an offer! Still in disbelief, they went inside the building and were speechless at what they saw. This wasn't just a factory: It was a kingdom of Poké Balls!

Poké Balls were everywhere. Some were displayed in glass cases, others ready to be sent out, and others still being created. The heart of the plant was an immense assembly line, with conveyor belts, mechanical arms, tanks, and all kinds of equipment.

"It's all automated!" Ash commented, noticing that there weren't any workers at the machines.

"Naturally," said the secretary. "Here, we use only the latest technology!"

"I'd love to observe the machinery up close!" said Clemont, his voice trembling with excitement.

"No need to rush!" cried the director. "We'll take you through all the phases of production—but first, we'd like to examine your Poké Balls."

"Why?" the friends asked, surprised by this strange request.

"We offer our visitors a unique service!" she replied.

"We verify any signs of damage, no matter how small, and repair them."

Clemont said eagerly, "Wow! It doesn't get better than that!"

"Just put them in here," the secretary said, opening a small briefcase. "We'll fix everything and return them to you as soon as possible."

The kids happily filled the briefcase, then Ash added, "There's just one problem. Pikachu doesn't like going into its Poké Ball."

"*Pika!*" Pikachu confirmed.

The deputy director then showed them a glass bell jar with a metal bottom. "You can put it in here."

Pikachu did not want to be stuck in that thing, but Ash reassured it as it climbed in. "Don't worry, it won't take long."

"Very good. Let's get going!" the secretary said, taking Pikachu's Poké Ball as well.

"Now," said the deputy director, "we'd like you to try out a special chamber that replicates the inside of a Poké Ball, so that you can feel what it's like to be a Pokémon."

"How fun!" cried Serena.

"Hooray!" shouted Bonnie, jumping for joy.

Their enthusiasm didn't last long. Even at first glance, the "special chamber" they were led to seemed bleak and dirty. Once the friends were inside, they saw it looked like an empty storeroom.

Before they realized that something wasn't right, a heavy metal door slammed shut behind them.

Ash reached for the doorknob. "Hey! Open up! What kind of game is this?"

"Pikaaa!" shouted Pikachu from the other side.

Ash peered out the window in the door and saw the trio of people start to sneer. A moment later, the so-called factory employees removed their masks. It was Jessie, James, and Meowth in disguise!

"Team Rocket?!" shouted Ash, gritting

his teeth with anger. How had he failed to recognize them?

"We're as surprised as you are," said Meowth, who had been the "secretary."

James nodded. "We were just minding our own business, stealing Poké Balls, when you turned up."

"So we decided to take Pikachu and all your Pokémon," Meowth concluded. "So there!"

"You won't get away with this!" shouted Ash. "Pikachu, Thunderbolt!"

"I'm sorry, but this container was specially built to resist electricity," Meowth said, cackling.

"*Piiii-kaaa!*" shouted Pikachu—and discovered that Meowth was right. But if it couldn't use electricity, it could still use its brain! The Pokémon quickly pushed its shoulders against the bell jar until it slipped out of James's hands and fell to the ground, breaking into a thousand pieces.

"Oops!" The trio from Team Rocket hadn't expected that.

"Now use Thunderbolt!" Ash shouted.

Pikachu attacked, but Jessie called on Wobbuffet, who returned the hit with Mirror Coat. Pumpkaboo and Inkay joined the battle using Shadow Ball and Psybeam, and the combination of these moves created a black cloud that enveloped Pikachu.

"Go on, go into your ball with no more funny business!" Meowth ordered Pikachu, moving the Poké Ball toward the cloud.

Ash could only watch helplessly. The beam from the Poké Ball traveled in the direction of Pikachu's shape, and when the cloud dissolved, the Mouse Pokémon had disappeared.

"Ha ha!" cried Meowth with great satisfaction.

"Nooo! Pikachuuu!" shouted Ash, beating his fists against the door. "You scoundrels! Give me back my Pikachu!"

Jessie, James, and Meowth sneered.

"So sorry," said James, "but we have every intention of keeping it!"

With that, the trio ran away to continue their evil plan, leaving Ash without a shred of hope.

At last they had succeeded. Team Rocket had taken Pikachu!

Now that there was no one to get in their way, the Team Rocket trio ransacked the Poké Balls at the factory. And not just the most common ones: The factory was

full of rare balls, such as the Great Ball, Ultra Ball, Dusk Ball, Net Ball, Premier Ball, and more. Jessie, James, and Meowth gleefully filled three big bags, stopping only when they were getting too heavy.

Meanwhile, in the storeroom, Ash was furious. However much he kicked and pounded on the door, it didn't give an inch.

He felt terribly guilty for having given Pikachu to Team Rocket with his own hands, and couldn't stand the thought that his friend was in danger. He was starting to lose hope of saving the Pokémon when he heard a familiar cry. *"Pika-piii!"*

It was Pikachu! It was in the hallway outside the storeroom.

"Pikachu!" cried Ash, beaming. "How did you get free?"

The Pokémon pointed to an air duct behind it. The grate that covered the duct was lying on the floor, and Ash understood what had happened.

"You weren't captured!" he said. "You took advantage of the smoke cloud and hid there!"

"*Pi!*" Pikachu confirmed.

"You're a genius, my friend," Ash said, laughing. "Now try to free us with Iron Tail!"

Pikachu nodded and hit the door with all its strength, again and again. However, there was little effect. It had probably been built to be Pokémon-proof.

Pikachu was still trying to use Iron Tail when Team Rocket turned the corner of the hallway. As soon as they saw the Pokémon, they panicked: that free Pokémon represented a setback as well as a danger to them.

"It's not possible!" cried Meowth, opening Pikachu's Poké Ball and finding it empty. "Come here, now!"

"Pikachu!" shouted Ash. "They don't have the briefcase anymore. Run and find it, and don't worry about us!"

Pikachu nodded and slipped into the air duct.

"Meowth!" shouted Jessie. "Where is the briefcase?"

"How should I know?" he replied. "I'll find it—and in the meantime, I'll get Pikachu. Now it's personal!"

With that, Meowth ran away, while his accomplices went to place the bags full of Poké Balls in the van they had waiting in the garage.

Meanwhile, Pikachu rushed through the air ducts and ended up in the part of the factory where conveyor belts moved the Poké Balls through different phases of production.

The briefcase was right there, forgotten in a corner. Pikachu jumped down from the air vent onto a conveyor belt and rode it toward the briefcase. But just when Pikachu was getting close, it realized it was suddenly moving backward!

It was Meowth's fault! He had pulled a lever to change the direction of the conveyor belt.

"Ha ha ha!" laughed the Scratch Cat Pokémon, taking hold of the briefcase. "Looking for this? Come and get it if you dare!"

Pikachu didn't need to be told twice: It charged right for him, but Meowth quickly extracted a Poké Ball with the intention of trapping it inside. Luckily, Pikachu had well-trained reflexes, and managed to escape before the beam could capture it.

At that point, a breathtaking chase began.

Pikachu rushed along the conveyor belt with Meowth at its heels. In addition to the devious Scratch Cat Pokémon, Pikachu had to deal with the mechanical arms that tried to grab it as if it were a Poké Ball. Meowth was no better off, and had to keep dodging the machinery, too.

At one point, Meowth was grabbed by a claw and pulled up high. Pikachu leaped up to grab on to the briefcase and try to take it away from him. But now both Pokémon were at the mercy of the machines. Passed on to other mechanical arms, they were soon transferred to the coloring section, where they began to be painted like Poké Balls!

That's when Jessie and James arrived. Faced with that ridiculous situation, they rushed to the control room to stop the machinery. But there was just one problem: Neither of them knew how to work the controls, and they ended up making things worse!

Meowth and Pikachu were passed from one painting station to the next. Finally, they were put through the polishing brushes, where they came out as shiny as marbles.

And in all the chaos of the chase, the briefcase had disappeared!

Back in the storeroom, Clemont tinkered with his tools and materials he'd found in the room. Finally, he got to his feet and announced, "The future is now, thanks to science! May I present the Extra Strength Pry-It-Open!"

The object he was referring to looked like a giant pair of pliers mounted on wheels. Clemont seemed very proud of himself as he explained how it worked. "Look here! We place the tip between the hinges then push the button, and the door will open!"

Ash, Bonnie, and Serena came closer to see the contraption in action. It began to exert strong pressure on the hinges. A few moments later, they noticed a burning smell, and suddenly . . .

BOOOM!

The invention exploded with a thunderous roar.

Even if it hadn't worked as planned, the Extra Strength Pry-It-Open had done its job: the door gave way in the explosion, and the friends were finally freed.

"Pikachu, I'm coming!" shouted Ash, rushing out of the storeroom.

Meanwhile, Pikachu continued to run away from Meowth, who kept trying to catch it with its Poké Ball. That Pokémon sure was stubborn!

"Those kids managed to escape!" shouted James, pointing to a monitor in terror. He could see footage of Ash and his friends on a security camera feed in the control room. It was definitely time for Team Rocket to leave the factory.

"Meowth, quick, let's scram! See you at the van!" shouted Jessie.

"After all this effort, I'm not giving up Pikachu!" he replied.

"Get a move on—we have to get going!" shouted James.

Against his every instinct, Meowth stopped chasing Pikachu. He spotted the briefcase moving along one of the conveyor belts and grabbed it before escaping.

Now Pikachu was starting to chase Meowth, but Ash's voice stopped it.

"Pikachu!" Ash shouted, appearing in the doorway. "I was so worried about you! I was afraid I'd lost you forever."

"*Pikaaa,*" his Pokémon replied, jumping into his arms. "*Pika, pika, pika,*" it added, nodding toward the exit where Meowth had disappeared.

"You're right. Let's go save our Pokémon friends!" Ash agreed.

The pair rushed out of the factory just in time to see the van emerge from the underground garage.

"We can't let them escape!" Ash cried. "Use Thunderbolt!"

Pikachu leaped off Ash's shoulder and unleashed one of its lethal Thunderbolts onto the van. The vehicle swerved and the back door flew open, causing all the stolen Poké Balls to spill onto the road. Jessie and James staggered out, stunned. Meowth, on the other hand, quickly recovered.

The Scratch Cat Pokémon skillfully climbed up onto the roof of the van and issued a challenge.

"Pikachu, if you want this briefcase, you'll have to face me in battle, one on one!" he announced.

By now, it was a question of honor for him.

"*Pika!*" replied Pikachu with determination. In a single leap, the Pokémon reached the van roof to face down its opponent.

"The winner will be decided with a single move," said Meowth.

The two Pokémon squared off. Pikachu waited to see what Meowth would do before acting. Meowth extended his claws and shouted, "Now you'll get a taste of my Fury Swipes!"

Pikachu immediately responded with Iron Tail, but Meowth had cheated: Behind his back, hidden in his tail, was a Poké Ball he could use to catch Pikachu once and for all. He had never really intended to battle Pikachu!

Pikachu, however, realized just in time. It barely avoided the beam, then gave Meowth a formidable hit with Iron Tail.

The Scratch Cat Pokémon fell to the ground in a faint, and the Poké Ball flew into Ash's safe hands.

Poor Meowth! It had gone badly for him—really badly.

Team Rocket had no choice but to flee, especially since reinforcements had arrived from the factory: Clemont, Bonnie, and Serena had found the actual factory employees, who Team Rocket had tied up, gagged, and locked in a room.

Pikachu and Ash hugged happily.

"My friend, you were fantastic as always!" the boy said.

"*Pikaaa!*" replied Pikachu.

"After all, as I well know," Ash added, thinking back to the rocky beginning of their friendship, "nobody can put my Pikachu into a Poké Ball!"

7

WHAT A MOVE!

Even heroes go on vacation from time to time, and Ash had the chance to do it in style. Thanks to Mr. Mime, Ash's mom had won a stay at an exclusive hotel on Melemele Island in the Alola region and had suggested that her son join her.

And so Ash had spent a few days relaxing and enjoying himself on the tropical island. He zipped across the clear waters on the back of a Sharpedo and discovered lots of Pokémon he had never seen before. That region was a true paradise!

Ash and his mom also had a small task to complete on behalf of Professor Oak: They needed to deliver a Pokémon Egg to his cousin Samson, a Professor who lived on the island. They were on the very street where Samson Oak's school was located when Ash had a little mishap.

His mom was at a fruit stand in the market, and Ash decided to wander around a bit. He saw a strange Bug-type Pokémon peeking out from a hole in the ground in a flower bed, and went to take a closer look. It didn't seem to be very friendly, though: As soon as Ash was within reach, it pinched his nose with its mandibles and then took off underground.

That got Ash's nose out of joint! He started to follow the Pokémon with the hope of catching it.

The creature was digging fast, and Ash hurried to keep up. After a long and fruitless chase, he found himself in the middle of the forest, and realized that he'd gotten completely turned around.

"We're lost!" Ash said to Pikachu. "How will we get back?!"

Looking around with the hope of finding the path back, the young Trainer noticed a rustling in the bushes. A moment later a large, cheerful Pokémon appeared, its arms open as if asking for a hug. Ash didn't know it yet, but it was a Bewear. And there was another thing he didn't know: Bewear can be very dangerous if they feel threatened. So when Ash stepped forward with the intent of making friends, the Strong Arm Pokémon let out a sharp squeal and then began breaking trees as if they were toothpicks thanks to the power of its paws.

"Aaaaaah!" shouted Ash, making a run for it. "What's with the Pokémon on this island?!"

With the Bewear at their heels, Ash and Pikachu ran and ran. When they reached the edge of the forest, they finally stopped to catch their breath, keeping an ear out in case the Pokémon was still following them. Luckily, the Bewear had decided to leave them alone and had returned to its den.

"We escaped!" Ash let out a sigh of relief. "But, what's that?" he added a moment later. He and Pikachu were on a hill with a spectacular view of the surrounding area, and an impressive structure lay before them. Its majestic buildings stood near the coast and were encircled by a canal.

"Let's check it out!" Ash suggested, and Pikachu jumped onto his shoulder.

But this was simply not their day. Ash had just climbed over the fence when they realized they were directly in the path of a racing herd of Tauros with Trainers riding them!

"WATCH OUT!" shouted a girl with long hair, standing at the edge of the track.

Too late. One of the Tauros ran right into Ash, and he ended up with his face in the dirt.

The girl riding it stopped immediately and turned around to help him. "I'm so sorry!" she said sincerely. "You popped out of the forest so suddenly that I didn't have time to stop!"

"It's my fault, don't worry!" said Ash, as he mentally checked all his bones to make sure everything was okay.

A small crowd of people had formed around him. In addition to the girl with the long hair and the one who had been riding the Tauros, a boy with a Togedemaru and another girl with a Popplio ran over, too.

"Hi, everyone," Ash said, a little embarrassed by all this attention. "My name is Ash. And this is my best friend, Pikachu. It's a pleasure to meet you!"

The others introduced themselves, too. The girl who had run into him was named Mallow, the one with the long hair was Lillie, Lana had the Popplio, and the boy was Sophocles.

"Welcome to the Pokémon School!" said Mallow. "I assume that you're lost. Come on, we'll help you find your way!"

Ash didn't even have a chance to respond before Mallow pulled him into the school. They went through large halls filled with prehistoric Pokémon fossils, classrooms full of students, libraries and reading rooms, and finally to a door marked "PRINCIPAL."

Mallow knocked politely and then cracked open the door.

"Good day, Mr. Principal," she said. "I'm here to introduce you to a new student."

"A new student?" said Ash. "No, wait, there's been a mistake!"

But before he could explain, Ash saw his mom—along with the principal, Professor Samson Oak! While Ash had been chasing Pokémon and dealing with the Bewear, his mom had gone to the school on her own and had already given the Egg to the Professor.

"Ash, you finally made it!" his mom said.

"Um ... I just had some minor delays," he explained.

Principal Oak shook his hand warmly. "Welcome!" He looked just like his cousin in Pallet Town, but he was decidedly more tanned and more ... lively. As Ash learned in the chitchat that followed, Samson Oak loved inserting puns involving the names of Pokémon into every sentence.

Once it was clear that Ash wasn't there to enroll, the kids took him on a tour of the school, leaving the adults to talk.

Ash was delighted: This place was a gold mine for anyone who loved Pokémon.

"We really learn a lot here," Mallow confirmed, as they admired their surroundings from a terrace.

A voice from below called out, "Hello there!"

"Hello, Professor Kukui!" Mallow replied, jumping up to greet the new arrival. He looked more like a champion of some kind of water sport rather than a teacher. This just confirmed Ash's suspicion that this was a very unusual school.

Mallow, Ash, and the Professor began to chat, but were soon interrupted by the roar of engines from outside. Three motorcycles stopped with a screech of brakes in front of the entrance, and two boys and a girl got off the bikes. All three were wearing matching bandannas around their faces and on their heads, and it was clear that they were there to cause trouble. Professor Kukui ran toward the entrance to figure out what they wanted, followed closely by Mallow and Ash.

In the courtyard, the teacher and the kids met up with Sophocles, Lillie, and Lana, who had also heard the sound of the engines. Meanwhile the three motorcyclists had walked up to a boy with spiky hair who was blocking their path along with a Charizard.

"How dare you?" one of the trio cried. "Team Skull doesn't let anyone get in their way."

"You're the ones getting in *my* way!" the boy replied boldly.

Ash asked his new friends, "Who are those guys? Do you know them?"

"Yes, unfortunately we know them well," replied Mallow. "That's Team Skull. All they do is bother people and cause trouble."

As if to confirm what Mallow had said, one member of the trio pointed at the boy with spiky hair and said sarcastically, "Maybe, if you beat us in a Pokémon battle, we won't do anything to you for once."

"But if we beat you," another one added, "your Charizard is ours."

"Great—I'll give you a real lesson!" the boy with spiky hair replied.

"That's what you think," the third member of the trio said, challenging him.

Without another word, the bad guys from Team Skull unleashed their Poké Balls all at once. And not even one at a time—each threw all three at once! And so three Zubat, three Salandit, and three Yungoos appeared in front of the boy!

"Stop this!" Ash shouted, running to stand alongside the boy. "This isn't a fair battle!"

"And what are you going to do? We're listening," said one of the Team Skull members.

"I'll fight, too," replied Ash. Then, turning to the boy with the spiky hair, he added, "If that's okay? Pleased to meet you—I'm Ash."

"I'm Kiawe," he replied. "Just try not to get hurt!"

Ash smiled. He liked this boy, who seemed almost as confident as Ash.

"Go on, Pikachu! I choose you!"

Kiawe sent the Fire- and Dragon-type Turtonator onto the field while Team Skull immediately began their attack.

"Salandit, show them your strength with Venoshock!"

"Yungoos, Bite!"

"Zubat, Leech Life!"

Ash cried, "Pikachu, Quick Attack!"

Pikachu engaged and sent the three Salandit into the air with a single strike.

"That speed!" Kiawe marveled. It's difficult for someone who has never seen Pikachu in action before to believe that such a small Pokémon could be so powerful!

Meanwhile, the Yungoos and the Zubat had launched

themselves at Turtonator only to be repelled and stunned by its Shell Trap, a move that made the spines on Turtonator's shell explode.

The Salandit attacked again, but Pikachu responded with Thunderbolt and knocked them out, too.

As the battle raged on, someone was peering through the tree branches, hidden from view. Two shining eyes stared at Ash, studying his every move.

Completely unaware of being watched from the shadows, the young Trainer cheered at Pikachu's good move. Ash was about to call out another instruction when Kiawe stepped up and announced, "I'll handle this now. This has gone on long enough!"

The boy crossed his hands in an X in front of his face. Flashes of bright light burst out of a wristband he was wearing and hit Turtonator. The Pokémon reared up on its hind legs and let out a deep growl.

"At the zenith of the mind, body, and spirit," shouted Kiawe as his body was surrounded by a fiery flame, "like the great mountain of Akala, become fire ready to burn! Inferno Overdrive!"

At those words, Turtonator created a gigantic white-hot sphere that floated for a moment in the air and then sped toward their opponents. The impact knocked the Yungoos, Salandit, and Zubat onto their backs.

The trio from Team Skull rushed to call their Pokémon back into their Poké Balls, then jumped onto their motorcycles, calling out one last threat as they sped off: "This isn't over!"

Ash was flabbergasted by what had happened. He had never seen anything like it. Kiawe wasn't limited to just giving commands to Turtonator: he could actively take part in the moves, as if he and the Pokémon were a single body.

"What . . . what was that?" he sputtered.

"It was a Z-Move," Professor Kukui explained. "They are special moves passed down in the Alola region that require a Z-Crystal and a Z-Ring. As you may know, this region is made up of four islands, and each of them has always been protected by a Legendary Guardian Pokémon. Only those who take part in a ceremony called the Island Challenge and complete it successfully can learn to use Z-Moves."

Pikachu looked at Ash and saw a familiar glint in his eyes. The Professor's words had made him want to get back on the road and participate in this intriguing Island Challenge!

Just then, Ash felt something fluttering around his head. He turned in time to see a creature fly past him and quickly disappear into the trees.

"What kind of Pokémon is that?" he asked.

"What Pokémon?" the others replied.

"What, didn't you notice it? It was right here!" said Ash, confused.

How could no one else have seen it? Ash was certain he hadn't just imagined it.

"It was yellow," he explained. "With an orange crest on its head!"

"Are you talking about *Tapu Koko*?!" cried Professor Kukui, in shock.

Lillie explained, "You just saw the Guardian of Melemele Island!"

"The Guardian of the island," Ash repeated, still a bit confused. He turned toward the forest, trying to make sense of his thoughts. Had the island's Guardian really shown itself to him? Why? Maybe it wanted to tell him something?

Those questions continued to swirl in Ash's head

the whole day, while everything he had seen at the Pokémon School played again and again in his mind's eye. At dinner that evening, he barely heard his mom chattering happily and asking him questions, which he answered distractedly.

At one point, Ash and Pikachu heard a strange cry. They went out onto the restaurant's terrace to find what had made the sound.

"It's that Pokémon again!" Ash said, seeing a yellow flash in the sky.

Without even a word to his mom, Ash jumped over the railing. He absolutely had to follow that Pokémon.

He and Pikachu rushed along the town's streets without running into anyone, neither humans nor Pokémon, until they found themselves in a town square. There they saw it: Tapu Koko floating in midair in front of them, looking very majestic.

Ash tried to calm down, because his heart was beating wildly. Then he dared ask, "Are you Tapu Koko? Can only I see you?"

The Pokémon raised a hand and let go of an object that swirled in Ash's direction. It was a wristband very similar to the one Kiawe wore.

Tapu Koko stared at Ash intently, then nodded. So the boy took the wristband, which began to sparkle, and he slipped it on his wrist as if it were the most natural thing in the world.

The Legendary Pokémon stared at him again for a moment, then turned and disappeared in a flash. Ash stood there under the starry sky, wondering about the significance of this mysterious gift.

The daily adventures, the atmosphere of the school on Melemele Island, and above all the prospect of learning so many new things had pushed Ash to make a decision. He would stay in Alola to take classes at the Pokémon School. His mother was happy with his plan—she knew it would be a wonderful experience for him.

So, after saying good-bye to his mom, Ash returned to the school to share the news with his new friends. They were delighted: Ash and Pikachu had already won them over. Only Kiawe seemed a little standoffish, as if he weren't sure what to think of him.

However, everyone was speechless when they saw Ash wearing the Z-Ring. It wasn't something you just picked up at the supermarket!

"Can I ask how you got an Electrium Z?" asked Kiawe. "I mean, you didn't participate in the Island Challenge."

"Electrium Z?" asked Ash, not understanding.

"That's what the crystal in the Z-Ring is called," Kiawe told him.

"Tapu Koko gave it to me!" Ash explained, looking at the band around his wrist.

"Did you really meet it?" Mallow asked, shocked.

"Yes! Pikachu and I heard its voice and followed its trail. When we found it, it floated down to us. It seemed to want to tell us something."

Professor Kukui, who was nearby, listened to Ash's tale very carefully.

"Then the Z-Ring came toward my hand, I put it on, and that's that!" Ash said simply.

The group let out an "oooh" of wonder, then Lillie

spoke. She said, "I heard that Tapu Koko is a Spirit Guardian that does all it can to help the islanders. But it also likes to play tricks on people—and if it thinks it's necessary, it can punish those who deserve it. I also read that, on rare occasions, it gives mysterious gifts to those it likes."

"That's fantastic!" Mallow said. "That means that Tapu Koko likes you, Ash!"

Ash realized the importance of the gift he'd received. "So that means that I could use a Z-Move!" he cried.

Kiawe was not as enthusiastic. "No! Z-Moves are not to be taken lightly. Only when the hearts of a Pokémon and its Trainer are perfectly in tune will the Z-Ring transform their feelings into power. But this bond must be used only for a special purpose."

"And what's that?" asked Ash, feeling ready for anything.

"To help those who are in need of it," replied Kiawe. "Only those who care about all the creatures of the world are able to use Z-Moves! I don't know what Tapu Koko saw in you, but from the moment you gained the Z-Ring, you were given a great responsibility."

"*Pika?*" asked Pikachu, as confused as Ash was.

Ash said to Kiawe, "I'm not sure I completely understand. But you can count on me." Then he added, chuckling nervously, "Sorry, I'm not really sure what else to say."

"I think that'll do!" Kiawe replied, and burst out laughing. In the end, Ash had won him over, too.

The next day, Ash woke up late. (Some things never change, in spite of all his adventures!) He ran to class, sure he'd be getting a lecture about being late, and instead was greeted by an explosion of confetti and a burst of applause.

"What . . . what's going on?" he asked.

"It's a surprise party!" his new friends cried.

"You weren't expecting it, huh?" said Kiawe.

"Definitely not!" Ash laughed.

"We thought that today would be perfect to have a welcome party for you," Mallow explained. "And now it's time for the best part!"

"What's that?" Ash was even more curious.

"Togedemaru and I want to challenge you!" Sophocles shouted, stepping forward.

Ash lit up. "You mean a Pokémon battle? Fantastic! Challenge accepted! Ready, Pikachu?"

He didn't have to wait for a response. *"Pika!"*

At hearing the word "challenge," Ash had already begun to imagine what his first move against an Electric- and Steel-type Pokémon like Togedemaru would be, but Sophocles had something completely different in mind.

Two small pools full of balloons were brought before the two challengers, and Mallow explained the rules. "The first team to pop all the balloons wins. It doesn't matter whether it's the Pokémon or the Trainer who bursts them. The important thing is not to miss a single one!"

It wasn't exactly the battle he had in mind, but Ash decided to try his best anyway.

"Okay!" he cried with his usual confidence. "This is child's play!"

But the game turned out to be harder than he'd anticipated. The balloons were made of a thick rubber, and popping them by squeezing them between your hands was difficult. Not even Pikachu's teeth, which were very sharp, could break them right away. At this rate, they'd be at this all day!

Togedemaru, on the other hand, had very sharp quills,

and all Sophocles had to do was place the Pokémon on top of the balloons and press gently to make them pop.

"You can use Pikachu's moves if you want!" Lana suggested.

"Great!" cried Ash. "Then let's break them all at once with Thunderbolt."

Sophocles grinned. That was just what he was expecting.

When Pikachu unleashed its move, the electric shocks went toward Togedemaru instead of the balloons. Sophocles shouted to his Pokémon, "Now use Zing Zap!"

The Roly-Poly Pokémon jumped into the pool and started to spin wildly. And a few moments later, it made all the balloons pop!

"Wait a minute, what happened?" asked Ash.

"Togedemaru has an ability called Lightning Rod," Sophocles replied. "It absorbs energy through its quills and can then release it in its next move. Isn't that great?"

"Cool!" said Ash. Even though he had lost, he was happy to have learned something, so he congratulated Sophocles on his win. This pleased the others, too, because it confirmed their impression of him: their new friend was a really great guy!

And someone else also liked Ash's attitude: Tapu Koko had been observing him in secret.

The party continued with other fun games. The next challenge was a swimming race between Lana's Popplio and Pikachu. Since Popplio was a Water-type Pokémon, it gave Pikachu a head start, but it won anyway without any trouble, flipping across the finish line.

Pikachu emerged on the shore a bit worse for wear, but Ash greeted it with a big smile. "Good job, my friend! You always give it your best try!"

Now it was Ash's turn, in a race against Kiawe, each on the back of a Tauros. A race that ended in a loss for Ash once again. But he didn't mind. He was enjoying himself, and was truly happy that his new friends had gone to the trouble of giving him such a warm welcome.

After all that activity, it was time for lunch. The kids sat around a table in the shade and Ash dug in. At one point, however, he heard a cry that was by now very familiar.

"Did you hear that?" he asked, getting up.

Then, something completely unexpected happened: Tapu Koko materialized in front of them! The Legendary Pokémon's eyes focused on Ash. It seemed to want to communicate something to him.

After Ash recovered from the shock, he smiled and said, "I'm happy to see you again. I haven't yet thanked you for the Z-Ring, so thanks!"

Tapu Koko let out a cry, then suddenly zoomed upward, flew behind Ash, and stole his hat! It had moved so quickly that it had practically been invisible.

The cap still in its beak, Tapu Koko stopped once again in front of Ash, then turned around and headed for the forest.

What could this all mean? Was it just a joke, or did it want to be followed? Considering that it had shown itself to be capable of extraordinary speed, its gentle flight away from the school seemed like an invitation.

In any case, Ash was determined to get back his hat, so he and Pikachu ran after the Legendary Pokémon, followed by the others.

After a long chase, Ash and Pikachu found themselves in a majestic clearing. The sunlight filtered through the trees, creating a play of shadows and reflections. It smelled of moss and mushrooms.

Tapu Koko descended from above, then put Ash's hat back on his head. So its action had in fact been a way of leading the boy here. But why?

"Do you . . . maybe want to . . . battle against me?" Ash asked, as the question entered his mind.

Tapu Koko took an attack position, showing that that was exactly what it intended. Ash felt proud. This was a great honor from a Legendary Pokémon!

"Okay," said Ash. "Are you ready, Pikachu?"

"*Pikaaa!*" it agreed.

Then Tapu Koko let out a sharp trill and began the match with Electric Terrain.

"Careful, Ash!" Lillie warned him as she arrived on the scene. "With Electric Terrain, Electric-type moves become much more powerful!"

"Good to know—thanks!" replied Ash. These were favorable circumstances, since he wanted to battle with Pikachu.

However, Tapu Koko pounced on Pikachu with such speed that the Mouse Pokémon was struck before it even knew what was happening. Pikachu was dazed for a moment, then ready to fight again.

"Let's show it what we can do," said Ash. "Use Thunderbolt!"

Pikachu's move surrounded Tapu Koko with an enormous burst of energy, but it didn't seem to do any damage to the Legendary Pokémon.

Professor Kukui was watching this incredible battle from the edge of the clearing with Kiawe, Lillie, Mallow, Sophocles, and Lana. "Tapu Koko is too strong for them," he commented.

Melemele's Guardian remained suspended in midair for a few moments, then sprang toward Ash. The boy covered his face with his hands, certain he would be struck, but Tapu Koko stopped a few inches from him and, with the tip of its hand, touched the Electrium Z on the boy's wrist.

At that gentle touch, the Z-Ring began to shine like a star.

Ash could tell right away—that gesture meant Tapu Koko was giving him permission to use the crystal's power!

"I have no idea how to do it, but I'll try!" Ash cried, observing the intense glittering at his wrist. "Go, Pikachu. Use our Z-Move!"

Ash recalled the movements he had seen Kiawe make and decided to imitate him. First, he crossed his hands in front of his face, then brought them to his sides, spread his legs for maximum stability, and held out his fist. Instinctively, Pikachu made the same movements as its Trainer.

The Mouse Pokémon's body was enveloped in a golden light, coursing with electricity. Then a large, luminous sphere appeared in front of it.

Pikachu and Ash moved their right arms backward and then forward as if to throw a punch. "This is it!" Ash shouted. "This is our maximum power!"

"Gigavolt Havoc!" Professor Kukui exclaimed, flabbergasted. "Incredible!"

The luminous sphere rushed toward Tapu Koko and exploded, making the entire valley shake. Everyone was forced to close their eyes to avoid being blinded by the flash, and held on tight to avoid being swept away by the impact. Meanwhile, a column of light rose to the sky.

The impact had been tremendous. Yet when Ash

opened his eyes, Tapu Koko was still there, undisturbed, hovering above the crater caused by the explosion. The only effect the Gigavolt Havoc had had was the destruction of the Electrium Z!

Tapu Koko raised its head, let out a cry, and zoomed upward, disappearing into thin air.

"Ash!" Mallow shouted, running over. "You're okay, right?"

"Yes," he replied, still feeling a bit out of it.

"That was incredible," the girl said. "I never imagined you and Pikachu could be so strong!"

"Well, I mean . . ." Ash chuckled, a little embarrassed by the compliment.

Kiawe brought him right back down to earth. "Did you see? Your Z-Crystal disintegrated. That means you're not yet ready to use Z-Moves. You haven't completed the Island Challenge!"

Ash lowered his head, feeling disappointed. But another feeling came to him, and his frown turned into a smile.

"All right," he declared. "That means I'll accept the challenge. I'll pass the test and get another Z-Crystal!"

"That's the spirit," Professor Kukui encouraged him.

Pikachu jumped onto Ash's shoulder, and Ash smiled at it. "Ready, my friend? Another great adventure awaits us!"

A battle between Pokémon (when it's not for evil purposes) is always fun and exciting. Pokémon love battling, especially when they have a Trainer by their side who's able to take advantage of their natural abilities. And there's no shortage of opportunities to be tested!

FRIENDLIES

Pokémon and their Trainers can battle without any purpose except to practice or to train before a competition. Ash, for example, never wastes

a chance to train with his friends! Here, his Oshawott is facing Cilan's Pancham.

GYM BATTLES

If a Trainer wants to participate in a region's Pokémon League, they must face the Gym Leaders: the people in charge of Pokémon Gyms. If the Trainer wins against a Gym Leader, they receive a medal. In general, Gym Leaders specialize in a specific type of Pokémon. Sometimes, Gym Leaders give their opponent an advantage by allowing them to use multiple Pokémon without ever changing their own. The only known region that doesn't have any Gyms is Alola.

BATTLES AND CHALLENGES BETWEEN POKÉMON

POKÉMON LEAGUE CONFERENCE

This kind of competition is one of the most important moments in the life of a Trainer. At a Pokémon League Conference, they have the chance to fight against Trainers and Pokémon that are very strong and well-prepared, and they can count on the support of a large crowd of spectators. To win, Trainers must pass the various elimination stages of the tournament and reach the final. Often, the final consists of a Full Battle in which each Trainer can use six Pokémon.

WORLD CORONATION SERIES

In the World Coronation Series, dreams can become reality. Whoever wins this competition is declared Monarch and can consider themselves the best in the world. Trainers from every region participate in this tournament—and obviously Ash is among them!

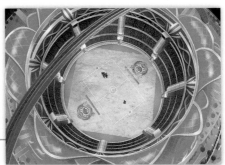

GALAR

BEST FRIENDS

What would be more exhilarating than watching a World Coronation Series final? Competing in it and winning, naturally.

The best Trainers from each region take part in this competition, and the battles are breathtaking. Whoever beats all the others receives the title of Monarch. They are the world champion, and they hold that title until the next tournament.

When Ash and his friend Goh were given tickets to the final match, held in the Galar region, they knew that they would be witnessing something unforgettable. The event surpassed their every expectation. The finalists were Lance from Kanto and Leon from Galar, and they faced off in an extraordinary battle during which their Pokémon assumed Dynamax and Gigantamax forms.

This meant that Lance's Gyarados and Leon's Charizard became enormous and used such powerful moves that the air all around them was filled with fire.

At the end of this battle between true giants, Leon won the title of Monarch. And the very moment he was declared the winner, Ash decided that sooner or later, *he* would battle Leon, too.

Meanwhile, this important tournament was unfortunately also an opportunity for people with evil plans—people such as Team Rocket.

Jessie, James, and Meowth were sent to Galar with the goal of capturing Pokémon that were capable of Gigantamaxing. That way, the band of villains would have the most powerful tools at their disposal to help carry out their plans for domination.

The trio had taken a break to watch the battle between Lance and Leon, and had left the stadium after the coronation ceremony to continue their hunt. Just as they reached the street, they ran into a Drednaw.

The Pokémon was taking a peaceful stroll and would gladly have avoided those three villains.

They noticed it right away, however! Jessie's Rotom Phone gave them all the information it had, which was very little. "Drednaw," the device recited. "The Bite Pokémon, a Water- and Rock-type, and . . . that's it, I don't know anything else!"

"Come on, nothing else?" Jessie said. "How come this thing never works right?"

Meowth studied the Drednaw. "It's a Pokémon from Galar," he said.

"So it could become giant, right?" added James.

They all agreed, "Okay, let's catch it!"

To kidnap the creature, Jessie launched Bellsprout from a Poké Ball. It did not seem like a good match to battle Drednaw, which looked much more threatening. However, the Flower Pokémon released a respectable Power Whip that hit Drednaw. When Bellsprout attacked again with the same move, though, Drednaw avoided the strike, and it hit the ground instead.

At that point, something completely unexpected happened: A column of energy shot up from the ground, surrounding Drednaw. Right in front of Team Rocket's terrified eyes, the Pokémon began to grow. And grow. And grow.

In just a few seconds, Drednaw had become a colossal Gigantamax!

The trio didn't waste any time wondering if they could still catch it. They knew right away that their only hope was to run away.

Unfortunately, out of all the directions they could have chosen to run, Jessie, James, and Meowth opted to take cover in the stadium, which was still jammed with spectators. Drednaw, full of rage and Gigantamax power, set after them with such determination that its head smashed one of the exterior walls into pebbles. The shock was felt throughout the stadium, and many spectators were thrown from their seats amid screams of terror. It was clear that something very serious was going on.

Ash and Goh exchanged a look and decided to do something about it. They didn't think twice about the trouble this could cause for them because their sense of responsibility was too strong. If there was danger, they needed to face it.

The two boys rushed outside and found themselves right in front of the Gigantamax Drednaw. The creature was truly terrifying, not just for its size but also because it had clearly lost control.

Once he was actually in front of it, Ash began to wonder what he could do against such a powerful Pokémon. The best thing that came to mind was simply talking.

"That's enough, now! Calm down!" he said. "You'll destroy everything!"

Drednaw stared at him with its enormous red eyes, and for a moment Ash thought that maybe his words had actually had an effect on it. But then he thought again, because the Pokémon let out a thunderous roar, its neck grew impossibly long, and the two boys found themselves just inches from its gigantic jaws.

"Aaaaaah!" Ash and Goh screamed.

That had been truly terrifying—the Pokémon's head was as big as a truck! But Ash quickly recovered from his fear and said with fists clenched, "Okay, all we can do is fight!"

"Huh?" said Goh in disbelief. Fight against a monster like that? Was Ash crazy?

"I know that we can't beat it," said Ash, as if he'd heard

Goh's thoughts. "But we have to attract its attention to get it far away from the stadium!"

"O-okay," Goh spluttered. "But what can we do against a Gigantamax Pokémon?"

"I don't know," Ash said with surprising honesty.

"You don't know?!" Goh replied.

"Something will come to me," Ash said, smiling. "You can step aside!"

"Forget it!" cried Goh, crossing his arms, offended. "If you fight, I fight, too!"

As this animated conversation continued, Drednaw was preparing its next attack. The rage it felt from Team Rocket's attempt to capture it had stirred it up like a volcano ready to explode!

"Use Thunderbolt, Pikachu!" Ash shouted, not wasting any more time.

Pikachu attacked and a powerful electric shock hit Drednaw right in the chest, but it didn't seem to have an effect.

"Double Kick!" Goh said to Scorbunny. The Rabbit Pokémon acted, but again Drednaw just blinked in response. Pikachu and Scorbunny seemed like gnats next to the Gigantamax Pokémon. The only effect their attacks had were to make the Bite Pokémon's rage even more incandescent. Its neck retreated to its shoulders and then plunged forward again. The boys were once again right up against its jaws, which were ready to bite.

"Use Electroweb!" Ash shouted.

Pikachu called up all its energy, and a web of electricity burst from its body toward Drednaw. This time, the Pokémon seemed to feel the attack and stopped its charge for a moment, but then it tore down the electric barrier and continued toward the boys. Ash and his friends took off, and Drednaw's head hit the ground with a crash.

Suddenly, a big crack appeared in the ground around Pikachu, and light started to filter up from below. After a few seconds, the Mouse Pokémon's tail began to crackle with electricity.

"What's going on?" Ash asked, in shock.

"I think I know," Goh replied, surprised.

Before Ash could ask Goh to explain, the answer came to life before his eyes. Pikachu's body began to grow and grow. It doubled in size, then tripled, and on and on . . . until the little Electric-type Pokémon had grown as tall as a ten-story building!

Ash looked on in disbelief. He had never suspected that his Pikachu was capable of something like that. But there was no doubt: it had become a Gigantamax!

Pikachu itself seemed confused. It was hard to recognize itself in that mammoth body, and every movement appeared to be hard to control. At one point, while trying to take a step, it almost trampled Ash and Goh!

"*Pi-ka, piii-kaaa,*" it said, in a deep, rumbling voice.

Drednaw, seeing such a huge opponent, reared up on its hind legs with the intention of charging. But Ash recovered in time to help Pikachu.

"Try Quick Attack!" he called.

Pikachu did its best to attack, but it wasn't easy to move quickly with so much bulk. Rather than being quick, its attack was very slow. It took one step at a time, trying to stay focused on not losing its balance. Drednaw took advantage of the pace and used G-Max

Stonesurge. Pikachu found that its path was blocked by
a geyser of rushing water.

Every movement made by the two enormous
Pokémon created strong vibrations all around them, and
a cry of fear rose up from the stadium. If the Gigantamax
Pokémon were to hit the building, it would be very bad
for the many spectators.

"There are still people inside!" Goh warned.

"Pikachu, use Iron Tail!" shouted Ash.

Now, at least, the two Pokémon were an even match.
All the same, executing Iron Tail was difficult because
Pikachu couldn't jump up and fall down on its opponent
from above as usual. So it took its tail in its hands and,
using it like a whip, beat it against the ground at its
feet. This move was called Max Steelspike, and it struck
Drednaw with the power of a gigantic steel blade.

"Yes, Pikachu! Good job!" shouted Ash, seeing the Bite Pokémon retreat.

Meanwhile, Leon ran out of the stadium and froze when he saw the unusual scene before him. Not only was there a Gigantamax Pikachu, but . . .

"That boy is in a Dynamax battle without a Dynamax Band!" he cried, seeing Ash. "How can that be?"

But Leon didn't have time to follow up. Drednaw had recovered quickly and now was unleashing a fearsome Max Rockfall, hitting the ground with its back legs. A tall rock rose up from the ground in front of Pikachu.

"What's that?" Ash wondered.

"It's a Rock-type Max move," replied Goh.

In spite of this information, Ash found himself at a crossroads. How should he react? What instructions should he give Pikachu?

Luckily someone came to his aid. "Tell it to use G-Max Volt Crash," a voice shouted. "I know that your Pikachu can do it!"

Ash turned toward the voice, and to his surprise, it was Leon! The Monarch was actually talking to him—and it was certainly worth listening.

"Great!" said Ash. "Pikachu, did you hear? Use G-Max Volt Crash!"

Drednaw crashed its head into the rock, but before it could fall onto Pikachu, the Mouse Pokémon leaped up, its body aglow with light. A column of pure energy shot up toward the sky. Initially, it seemed as though nothing had happened, then the clouds were split by a flood of electricity that attacked the rock and Drednaw. The Bite Pokémon fell backward, and immediately its body shrank until it was back to its normal size.

Soon after, Pikachu also returned to normal size, and Ash ran over and hugged it.

"Pikachu, you were amazing!" he said, holding his partner close. "As always, you made the best of the situation!"

"Are you okay?" asked Leon, running over to them.

"Yes, everything's fine!" said Ash. "Thank you for the advice. I needed it!"

"I'm the one who should be thanking you," said Leon. "You showed great courage, and you saved everyone in the stadium! May I ask what your name is?"

Ash's heart swelled with pride. "I'm Ash Ketchum from Pallet Town," he replied.

"And I'm Goh from Vermilion City."

"I'm Leon," said the Monarch, as if he needed to introduce himself.

"We all know you!" said Ash. "Speaking of which, I have a favor to ask."

"No, please, don't," Goh interrupted, guessing what his friend had in mind.

But Ash continued anyway. "Would you consider a battle against me?"

Goh gulped with embarrassment. He couldn't believe Ash was so bold.

Leon, however, didn't seem to mind. After a moment of surprise, he smiled and winked at Ash.

Proposal accepted!

The next day, Ash and Leon met in Wyndon Stadium for a truly unusual battle. Normally, those who face the Monarch must make it through a difficult battle process made up of several elimination rounds before reaching the final round. The fact that Leon had agreed to participate in a friendly match was truly exceptional, due to the extreme courage shown by Goh and Ash in facing the Gigantamax Pokémon—and also Ash's courage in proposing the battle.

Goh still couldn't believe it was really happening.

And yet, right before his eyes, Ash and Leon really were there at the center of the immense battlefield, ready to go.

"Here, take this," said Leon, handing Ash a white wristband with a strange red symbol.

Ash took the object and studied it with interest.

"That's a Dynamax Band," Leon explained. "I noticed that you don't have one yet, but it's essential for having full control over Dynamaxing. The move names change for Dynamax Pokémon, too."

"Yes, I know about that," Goh said. "The Normal-type Max move is called Max Strike, the Steel-type one is called Max Steelspike, and the Electric-type one is called Max Lightning."

It was all completely new for Ash! But he wasn't discouraged.

Pikachu was there on his shoulder, as always, and that gave him an infinite sense of security. Together, they could learn to manage the new moves and whatever other challenges arose.

"And of course Pikachu is able to Gigantamax," Leon said. "And it can use the Electric-type Max move that defeated Drednaw, the G-Max Volt Crash. When you want to go Dynamax, you need to put your Pokémon back in its Poké Ball, and then you have to let it focus its energy into the Dynamax Band."

"To be honest, Pikachu doesn't really like staying in its Poké Ball," Ash said. "We might have to come up with something different."

"*Pika, pika!*" Pikachu agreed.

"Well, put on your wristband and get ready," said Leon with a smile. "You know I have no intention of going easy on you!"

"That's what I was hoping for!" Ash replied. "Come on, Pikachu, let's go!"

While Goh moved out of the arena, Pikachu leaped onto Ash's shoulder and got in position. Leon, for his part, sent Charizard into the field—the Pokémon that had helped him win the title of Monarch the day before.

"Wow!" cried Ash. "Pikachu and I were hoping to fight against Charizard!"

"I see you understand your Pokémon well!" Leon noted. "That makes me happy!"

Ash blushed at the well-deserved compliment. Now he was ready to prove himself on the field of battle!

"Pikachu, Quick Attack!" he cried.

"Charizard, counterattack with Thunder Punch!" shouted Leon.

Pikachu attacked the Flame Pokémon with all its energy, but Charizard was extraordinarily powerful. Its Thunder Punch completely canceled out the Quick Attack.

Ash told Pikachu to attack again, this time with Iron Tail, but once again it was easily rebuffed by Thunder Punch. Not even its Electroweb could resist Charizard's super-powerful move, and Charizard counterattacked with Air Slash. Poor Pikachu was enveloped in a flurry of blades of light, but it didn't retreat an inch.

"Good job!" shouted Ash. "Now use Thunderbolt!"

Pikachu got ready to make a big strike, but found that Charizard was ready with a Flamethrower. Its fire overwhelmed and surrounded the Mouse Pokémon. For a long moment, Ash watched his Pikachu engulfed in flame.

He was thinking about pulling out of the match when

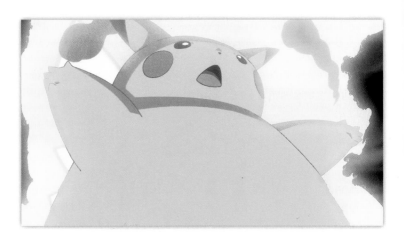

something happened. His Dynamax Band flashed, and beams of light stretched out toward Pikachu. Then his Pokémon began to grow!

"We did it without a Poké Ball!" Ash cheered. Evidently, the strength of his love for Pikachu was enough to activate the wristband.

"Incredible! I'm so glad to witness this!" said Leon. Even though he was very experienced, he was still moved to see the power of the bond between Pokémon and their Trainers.

Leon held a Poké Ball out to Charizard and called it inside, then announced, "Now wait and see!"

The Poké Ball lit up with purple light. Leon unleashed it, shouting "Gigantamax!"

The Charizard that erupted from within was mammoth-sized. Tall flames licked around its face and shoulders, and its roar made the stadium shake.

"Go, Pikachu," Ash called. "Time for Max Strike!"

Pikachu stomped on the ground, and a torrent of energy exploded from the cracks it created.

"Use Max Airstream!" Leon shouted to Charizard.

Air swirled from Charizard's jaws, making Pikachu fall to the ground. But it wasn't time to stop yet.

"Pikachu, use Max Steelspike!" Ash cried.

"Charizard, use Max Lightning!" Leon yelled.

Charizard's countermove stopped Pikachu from finishing its move, but Ash was determined to try everything.

"G-Max Volt Crash!" the boy shouted.

Pikachu repeated the move it had used the previous day against Drednaw, and this time it knew what it was doing. A column of energy extended upward, ready to pour down on Pikachu's opponent. But Leon wasn't just twiddling his thumbs, and instructed Charizard, "Use G-Max Wildfire!"

So, even as the energy generated by the G-Max Volt Crash hit Charizard, a fiery inferno surrounded Pikachu.

It tried to resist as long as it could, but Charizard's move was unstoppable. Soon the Mouse Pokémon's body began to shrink, and it quickly returned to its normal state.

The battle was over—Pikachu was in no shape to continue.

Ash ran to take the Pokémon in his arms. "You were great," he praised it. Pikachu slowly opened its eyes.

Leon approached and handed him an Oran Berry. "Take this," he said. "It will help your Pokémon recover quickly."

"Thanks a million," Ash said. After making sure that Pikachu had eaten the berry, he added, "I'm very glad that you didn't go easy on us in the battle."

"There's no point in battling if you're not going to give it your all," replied Leon.

Ash nodded. He took off the Dynamax Band and handed it back, saying, "Thank you for loaning this to me!"

"No, take it!" said Leon. "You have much to learn as a Trainer, but I like your style. If you want to beat me, though, you still have a lot to do. You need to stand out!"

Then the Monarch turned to leave, but first added, "Next time, I'll see you in an official competition!"

"Okay!" said Ash, already looking forward to it.

When Goh rejoined him, Ash declared, "I decided to sign up for the tournament."

"I'm not surprised!" Goh replied, laughing.

Ash burst out laughing, too. His passion for battles wasn't exactly a secret.

Meanwhile, Pikachu had completely recovered. It hopped onto Ash's shoulder—its favorite place in the world.

"You know, Pikachu," the boy said, giving the Pokémon a bright smile, "even when you're not Gigantamax size, you're truly special!"

"*Pikaaa,*" said Pikachu, patting his cheek.

"As special as your friendship," Goh said. "Ash and Pikachu, friends forever!"

THE ADVENTURE DOESN'T END HERE!

WITH NEW CHALLENGES, NEW FRIENDS, AND NEW POKÉMON . . .

ASH AND PIKACHU CAN
ALWAYS COUNT ON
EACH OTHER!

POKÉMON BOOKS!